For fourteen years now *Perry Rhodan* has been acknowledged to be the world's to series. Originally publish the series has now appea the States.

Over five hundred *Perry R* Continent and *Perry Rhoda* annually. The first *Perry Rh* *Space*, has now been released in Eu

The series has sold over 150 million copies in Europe alone.

Also available in the *Perry Rhodan* series

ENTERPRISE STARDUST
THE RADIANT DOME
GALACTIC ALARM
INVASION FROM SPACE
THE VEGA SECTOR
THE SECRET OF THE TIME VAULT
THE FORTRESS OF THE SIX MOONS
THE GALACTIC RIDDLE
QUESTION THROUGH SPACE AND TIME
THE GHOSTS OF GOL
THE PLANET OF THE DYING SUN
THE REBELS OF TUGLAN
THE IMMORTAL UNKNOWN
VENUS IN DANGER
ESCAPE TO VENUS
SECRET BARRIER X
THE VENUS TRAP
MENACE OF THE MUTANT MASTER
MUTANTS VS MUTANTS
THE THRALL OF HYPNO
THE COSMIC DECOY
THE FLEET OF THE SPRINGERS

Kurt Mahr

Perry Rhodan 23: Peril On Ice Planet

Futura Publications Limited
An Orbit Book

An Orbit Book

First published in Great Britain in 1977
by Futura Publications Limited

DEDICATION

This English Edition
Dedicated to
HAL CLEMENT
Whose 'Iceworld'
Became an Instant
Classic in 1951

Series and characters created and directed by Karl-Herbert Scheer and Walter Ernsting, translated by Wendayne Ackerman and edited by Forrest J. Ackerman.

ISBN 0 8600 7941 4

Printed in Great Britain by
Cox & Wyman Ltd,
London, Reading and Fakenham

Futura Publications Limited
110 Warner Road, Camberwell
London SE5

CONTENTS

Perry Rhodan 23:
Peril on Ice Planet

CHAPTER ONE

SPRINGERS *VS.* THE *SOLAR SYSTEM*

Space quaked as the structure sensors in Perry Rhodan's command centre registered transition after transition.

Each hyperjump caused a disturbance in the fabric of the space-time continuum sufficient that sensitive instruments could record the results.

In this case, however, the distances were not especially great: the ships emerging from the transitions at moderate speeds were only between 7 and 21 light-years away.

But the continuum rendings had been continuing for half an hour and the situation was beginning to become acute for the three Earthships hovering motionless in space, 8 light-years from the centre of gravity of the Beta–Albireo constellation. Three gigantic spherical ships – *Terra* and *Solar System*, each measuring 600 feet in diameter, and the 2500-foot *Stardust*. The only three *large* units of the Terranian Space Fleet, under the command of Perry Rhodan.

Rhodan himself had taken over as First Pilot of the *Stardust* and the battleship was fully manned and ready for action. Reginald Bell assisted him as

Second Pilot and Fire Control officer. The operators of the most important communication equipment were doubled.

The very air of the command centre seemed to pulsate with tension. There was actually little danger that the three Terranian ships could be detected, for the usual rangefinders were reliable only up to a distance of two light-years at most; still, it was possible that one of the Springer ships might stray into their sector by accident and run into the nervous outnumbered Earthships.

One of the younger officers was busy checking the quantity of transitions as accurately as possible. Rhodan wanted to know how many opponents they would have to contend with if worst came to worst.

'Seventy-eight, sir!' the young officer replied nervously. 'But there seems to be a letup at the moment.'

Bell spun round. 'I don't like it,' he growled in a tone low enough so that only Rhodan was able to hear him.

Rhodan shrugged his shoulders. 'Nobody asked us,' he observed. 'Besides, so far we run little risk. It's not likely that one of their ships will stumble on us.'

The pause lasted surprisingly long. Rhodan began to think that the 78 units the adversary had brought in were all he planned to use for the imminent battle. Then the transturbulence started again.

This time the Springers came from a different direction and the mean distance of the transitioning ships was around 38 light-years. There was no doubt that it was a second group of hostile ships but Rhodan didn't know what their connection with the first one was.

The young officer counted 90 new transitions. Now they had to contend with 168 fighting ships!

Rhodan observed grimly, 'They're not satisfied with halfway measures! They've mustered almost six times as many ships as on the first try.'

Bell twisted his face into a broad grin. 'They've got respect for us!' he asserted.

Rhodan gave no answer. For a while he just stared silently. Suddenly he spun around and looked Bell in the eyes. 'You've to get out there, Bell!' he said tersely.

Bell was not surprised. 'I thought so,' he replied. 'Because of Tifflor, isn't it?' Then he smiled and boasted with obvious pride: 'You couldn't have found a better man!'

'Because of Tifflor – *and* the approaching enemy,' Rhodan added. 'We must have information on the spot in order to find out what the intentions of the Springers are.'

'Okay. And how do we proceed?'

Rhodan was ready with a plan. He answered without hestitation: 'I'll give you Lieutenant Everson and the K-6. The K-6 will hytrans to reach the target area. As soon as the transition's completed you'll leave the ship in a destroyer. The robot storageroom contains everything Tifflor and his men will need. Pucky will accompany you . . .'

'Pucky!' Bell groaned.

'. . . and transfer the provisions by teleportation to the surface of the planet. Pucky must be given strict instructions that the job from the time of leaving the K-6 to the moment he jumps off *cannot* take more than half a minute. All you have left to do is return on the shortest way.'

'In the destroyer?' Bell snapped.

'Right! Everson and the K-6 will transback the minute you leave. We can't afford to risk any more Guppies.'

'I get the impression,' Bell said slowly with a sad smile, 'you want to get rid of me. But I suppose there is no other way.'

Rhodan made a wry face.

'I've racked my brains for the last half hour but I couldn't come up with anything better.'

'A lot of movement, sir,' Aubrey piped up.

His voice appeared to be full of concern but naturally this was not the case at all. Because Moses, whose official name was RB-013, was incapable of feeling apprehension or any other emotion for that matter. Aubrey was a fighter-robot of Arkonide origin and had acquired his nickname only a few hours earlier.

It had been given to him by the three cadets and two girls from the Space Academy with whom he had arrived in an incapacitated destroyer which had cracked up completely while landing on this planet. They had come but a short time ago to this world which circled the two suns of the Beta–Albireo system in an eccentric orbit and was at the present time more than seven astronomical units away from the light-giving centre of the system. Its surface was covered with an infinite expanse of ice and snow and its mean temperature had sunk to minus 170° F.

The three cadets were Julian Tifflor, Klaus Eberhardt and Humphry Hifield. Mildred Orsons and Felicita Kergonen were the two girls. They had fled to this world in a destroyer because they escaped from the auxiliary ship K-7 when it was threatened by the enemy. During their flight the destroyer was shot up and lost its manoeuvrability. The icy world was the only place close enough to risk a landing.

The destroyer was smashed in the emergency landing. The crew of five and Aubrey, the robot, had suffered no damage. They marched a few hundred miles south to reach a warmer zone and managed to wrest from their pursuers a two-man patrolship which had been sent out to capture them.

As long as the enemy had only one ship available, the ORLA XI, the situation was not too dangerous. Tifflor – Tiff for short – and his people had sufficient provisions for two years. The cave into which they had retreated sheltered them from the icy cold of the alien environment. The conquered patrolship was so well concealed in a nearby mountain cleft that it could only be detected by being directly on top of it.

Now, however, their situation appeared to be changed. Aubrey registered on his instruments the movements of several ships. As Aubrey's rangefinder had only a limited range, it meant that the ships were already fairly close. Doubtlessly, they were interested in this planet.

They were interested because they suspected that

one of the five was a person of the highest importance.

Tiff, who had assumed leadership of the small group because he demonstrated the most competence, faced a difficult decision. The cave in which they were hiding out was not far enough away from the place where they had discovered the patrolship and it was, therefore, liable to be detected in a search organized by his foes.

However, to change their position now would have meant exposing to the rangefinders of their opponents the considerable mass of metal of which the robot consisted.

Tiff considered this to be the greater hazard and decided: 'We'll stay right here for the time being.'

Nobody raised objections, not even Humphry Hifield who seldom passed up an opportunity to quarrel with Tiff.

'Ready to take off!' Lieutenant Everson bellowed.

The response was considerably calmer: 'Ready! Clear out!'

Everson pressed the switch. The hatchdoors of the large auxiliary ship hangar slid apart at maximum speed. The auxiliary ship K-7 departed slowly. The black sky with its multitude of stars appeared on the observation screen.

Everson spoke into the intercom mike: 'We're outside, sir! We'll make the jump in two minutes.'

Reginald Bell's voice sounded nonchalant. 'Very good. Go ahead, Lieutenant!'

Bell was already at his post. He sat in the pilot seat

of the little destroyer which the K-7 carried in its hangar.

In two minutes the K-7 would proceed with the transition and emerge at practically the same moment in the target area since the jump was performed without measurable time delay. Within a second the Z-13 was scheduled to leave the hangar and half a minute later the first part of the perilous job would be finished.

In the second seat of the three-man cockpit sat Pucky.

Bell had to admit that he'd never got used to Pucky even though they'd been together more than a year – more than five years by Terrestrial time concept, taking into consideration the four years that had somehow been lost among the stars on a trip with Rhodan and his crew in the super-spaceship.

Of course there were good reasons why it was difficult to get used to Pucky.

Pucky looked like a cross between a beaver and a mouse. His body was about three feet long and covered with reddish brown fur. He had the plump hindpart of a beaver and big ears like a mouse. In spite of his appearance Pucky was an intelligent being. In addition to his own language he spoke English with a slight accent and a lisp. Furthermore, he possessed an amazing variety of parapsychological capabilities, including telepathy, teleportation and telekinesis.

'Have you made contact with Tiff?' Bell asked.

Pucky nodded in the most refined human manner. 'Yes, I'm in constant touch with him,' he replied.

Cadet Tifflor carried within his body – without being aware of it – a highly active cell transmitter which turned him into a sort of telepathic beacon. Efficient telepaths like Pucky were able to spot Tiff from a distance up to two light-years.

Bell wanted to ask something else but didn't get a chance. Lieutenant Everson's loud voice droned from the loudspeaker: 'Attention, transition! Ten . . . nine . . . eight . . .'

Bell concentrated and his hand grasped the drive lever on the instrument panel. The airlock was set to open automatically after the transition.

'. . . four . . . three . . . two . . . one . . . go!'

The peculiar pain of de-materialization, a feeling of having their limbs torn apart, set in, but this time it passed so quickly that their brains had barely time to perceive it.

When Bell opened his eyes again the Z-13 was already out in space and had left the K-7 far behind.

His hand had pushed the lever forward with a trained reflex. The Z-13 accelerated at maximum and the faint speck of light that was the grey globe where Cadet Tifflor and his people had sought refuge, grew on the picture screen.

All this seemed to mean nothing to Pucky. He showed no apparent interest as he sat in his seat. His usually big trusting eyes were narrowed to small slits.

Pucky focused in on the target. Thirty seconds was not much time to pinpoint the range. He failed to hear Bell's angry shout:

'What in blazes is going on here? The sky is loaded with Springers!'

Near the light-grey curvature of the icy planet a swarm of glimmering points was visible.

Ships! An entire fleet of hostile ships!

Bell knew that there were only two facts in his favour: the element of surprise which the appearance of the little destroyer was bound to cause among his adversaries and his manoeuvrability which excelled that of the huge Springer ships.

The sphere of the strange planet grew larger than the frame of the observation screen and the alien ships became dark spots against the light background as they gained in size and took on shape.

'Go, Pucky!' Bell growled. 'We'll soon be under fire! They really must have been caught by surprise since they haven't started shooting yet.'

Pucky chirped in reply: 'Now!'

When Bell turned his head half a second later to look at him, he had already vanished and with him several loads weighing three tons on Earth – made portable by an antigrav-generator.

Bell took a deep breath and changed the course of his machine abruptly. A faint green ray of concentrated energy discharged from one of the dark spots made by the Springer ships against the snowscape in the background. It shot into space and crossed the course the Z-13 had just left at the spot where it would have been if Bell hadn't taken evasive action.

The turn had shifted the picture of the cold planet to the edge of the optical screen.

Z-13 headed – within one arc second – straight for the dwarf star which was one of the two suns of the dual system.

Reginald Bell held his course for two minutes, then pulled his machine around again groaning under the pressure he suffered as the radial acceleration exceeded the value which could be compensated by the neutralizer in the destroyer.

The turn amounted to a few degrees only but it took place at top speed in an extremely short time interval and it caused the enemy's second energy bundle to miss. The shot spent itself harmlessly far off in space.

But Bell noticed on the panoramic observation screen that there was movement in the hostile fleet in his rear.

Three of the ships picked up speed and began to pursue the Z-13.

Bell scowled when he checked the rangefinder instruments.

The three ships were of cylindrical shape with pointed ends built like all Springer ships and one of them was 2500 feet long.

A gigantic spaceship! Although smaller than the mighty *Stardust*, it outclassed the tiny Z-13 in every respect.

Bell began to realize that he would need help to save his skin in the impending pandemonium.

He aligned his hypercom antenna with the position of the three Terrestrial spaceships and sent out the message in a gruff voice:

'Daisy is freezing!'

Alarm whistles shrilled through Etztak's colossal spaceship.

Etztak, the patriarch of the Orlgans clan, was in the command centre when the rangefinder sounded the alert.

Etztak was very old – even old for a Springer. He was over six and a half feet tall, a giant stooped under the burden of his years. The white waves of his magnificent beard rolled down on his chest and his head of hair grew no less luxuriantly.

'What's the matter?' Etztak's voice boomed.

The rangefinder reported meekly: 'A foreign object has appeared, Lord! Approaching our position at great velocity!'

'What kind of ship?' Etztak shouted.

'Not a ship, Lord! Too small for that. It's one of the craft the strangers carry on board *their* ships.'

Etztak panted in rage. 'Open fire at once!'

And so that the other ships of his clan would receive instructions he hit the switch of the hypercom so hard that it almost broke. 'Full firepower on the unknown target!'

Etztak's word was command. The reason his order was not immediately fully complied with was that at the moment it was given only two other ships besides Etztak's own had spotted the enemy.

Etztak's ship ETZ XXI was the first to fire. The shot missed its mark because the target had executed a daring turn a fraction of a second earlier.

Fifteen seconds later WENA LXIII, the neighbour ship of ETZ XXI, had its guns ready to fire. It discharged a disintegrator salvo on the tiny point which raced at incredible speed past the ice planet in the direction of the blue-white sun. But as if all the devils in the universe were helping the stranger, he changed his course again at the right moment and sped away without a scratch.

Etztak was informed about the developments as soon as they happened.

Now he was in his element! The fight had broken out and at such a time his whole clan had to obey him alone. He directed his people to remain with most of the ships close to the surface of the ice planet and took up the pursuit with the ETZ XXI, WENA LXIII and HORL VII.

Etztak's instructions were simple: 'The alien craft must be destroyed under all circumstances!'

Eight light-hours away the hypercom antenna of the *Stardust* picked up the radio message: 'Daisy is freezing!'

Perry Rhodan had expected the situation to become serious. It would have been incredible luck if Bell could have penetrated the ranks of the enemy without trouble.

Rhodan advised the *Solar System* under Major Nyssen's command: 'Get ready for a transition, Nyssen. Use your special antenna and watch for Bell's code-signal . . . if it comes at all. Take your bearings with the antenna and proceed as quickly as possible. I depend on you to do a good job. Bell seems to be in a nasty fix.'

Nyssen accepted the order and added in an angry tone:

'We'll show 'em, sir!'

Bell's brain worked in high gear. The question was when it would be the most opportune time to notify Rhodan that Daisy was already half dead in the freeze.

That moment was no longer very far off.

The 2500-foot-long spaceship proved its ability to beat the Z-13 with its acceleration powers. From a dead start and an unfavourable position, the enormous spaceship managed to gain in a few seconds almost the same speed as the little destroyer.

The two other vessels fell a little behind the giant ship but Bell little doubted that they too could become a very serious threat over a long stretch.

Bell had already given up his plan to return to the *Stardust* by the shortest way. To do this he would have to fly in a 180° curve and this would have driven him directly into the arms of the enemy.

But Bell was not a man to throw in the towel. He knew that the Z-13 had one critical advantage over the colossal ship menacing him: its superior manoeuvrability. The crucial time for the Z-13 would arrive when the attacker approached within 3000 miles.

However, that moment would never come if his formidable pursuer were to decide to start shooting from a greater distance.

The unbearably bright light from the blue dwarf sun had wandered out to the right of his observation screen. The dimmer orange-coloured blotch of the main sun shone from the corner of the screen and bathed the little cockpit in a pleasant yellow light.

How nice it would be, Bell thought.

That's when the alarm sounded again. 'Ships at twelve o'clock!'

Bell saw on the rangefinder panel once more the glittering swarm of 90 spaceships whose transition he had observed on board the *Stardust* one hour and a half before.

The Z-13 aimed straight at it. With an angry expletive Bell gave his little craft another twist to the left. Although it brought him closer to the powerful enemy chasing him, he could thereby evade the menace of 90 more warships . . .

Bell stopped short in the middle of the thought. *Tommyrot!*

Another change of course and back to the old flight direction! What greater security could there be than seeking cover between the enemy's own ships!

After Etztak had followed the careening course of the strange craft for a few minutes he thought he had seen the weirdest pilot ever.

'Look at him!' Etztak shouted and all eyes followed him obediently to the rangefinder screen. In the luminous substance the path of the hunted was traced like the tail of a comet.

'What does he think he's doing, weaving from left to right?' the patriarch's voice thundered. 'Does he really believe he can get away from us this crazy way?'

Etztak got his answer from the rangefinder technician: '90 units of our battle fleet straight ahead, Lord! Distance seven light-minutes!'

Etztak saw the points appear on the screen. The antenna followed their movements and depicted them on the screen as standing motionlessly which was the actual case with respect to the centre of the system.

And that midget – that ridiculous brazen midget – headed straight for the armada! Etztak realized that he had to act at once: 'Fire broadside!'

But the Springers were not trained to react instantaneously and precisely to an order which came a few minutes earlier than they had been led to expect. Shortly after the beginning of the pursuit Etztak had become aware that the acceleration potential of the strange craft was inferior to the ETZ XXI and had therefore issued strict instructions to open fire only after the distance had been reduced to less than 18,000 miles.

Everybody was familiar with Etztak's reasoning. A shot from such a short distance would turn the stranger into a flaming torch of exploding gas, a lesson for all who dared oppose the Springer clan of Orlgans.

It would have been a fine spectacle of the kind Etztak loved dearly. Then why did the old man withdraw his orders now? What had happened to change his mind?

Nobody knew. The fire control officers were confused and the long barrels of the energy weapons slowly tracked their target.

'Daisy is already half dead!' Bell relayed.

The Z-13 took a short painful leap upwards and

went back to the same course again after a few seconds.

Not a shot was fired. The gun turrets of the ETZ XXI were still busy homing in on their prey and Bell's aerobatic evasive leap had been superfluous.

'Okay,' Nyssen said calmly. 'I heard you! *Solar System* ready for transition!'

The *Solar System* vaulted into hyperspace from a standing start without attaining the velocity which was normally a prerequisite for a transition. The ship jumped with an energy discharge of unimaginable proportions. The five-dimensional explosion, invisible to the human eye, hurled the *Solar System* into hyperspace.

Nyssen felt the stinging pain and lost consciousness for a fraction of a second. When he recovered again the *Solar System* had landed in front of the glittering hostile ships.

The Z-13 showed as a tiny speck on the rearview screen not far from the thin elongated body of a vessel.

Nyssen was as startled as Bell a few minutes previously when the sensors delivered the result of the measurements: 'The ship is cylindrical with torpedo-shaped ends. Length 2500 feet, diameter 250 feet.'

It was plain to see from Nyssen's position that the only imminent danger to the Z-13 came from the gigantic ship. All the others were still outside the usual range of energy rays.

'All battle stations ready to fire!' Nyssen shouted into the microphone.

The response was immediate. The cannons had already been manned before the *Solar System* went into transition.

Nyssen lost no time and rushed towards the tiny racing point and the even faster long ship on the prowl.

'Distance 4.13 light-seconds!'

Bell's instruments registered the *Solar System* the same moment it emerged and he sighed with relief.

Not that he believed that all his troubles were over. The *Solar System* was at the moment of its appearance still too far away to join the impending clash. But at least he was no longer alone. If he could manage to out-manoeuvre the Goliath for a few more seconds, the *Solar System* would arrive on the scene.

Bell did his best.

And Etztak wished all the powers of darkness on his Earth adversary.

The turret guns were all trained on the target with perfection. Shot after shot was loosed from the funnel-shaped gun muzzles. Some blasted through space with a flash, others with a faint glimmer or completely invisible, in the all-out effort to blow up the little machine.

However, even the best of aiming mechanisms involved some lost motion. It took a few thousandths of a second to align the heavy gun barrels again in the new direction but this tiny interval was enough for a machine with the agility of the Z-13 and its superb thrust-absorbers to perform a turn of more than five degrees.

The ray-shots from the ETZ XXI all whizzed by the Z-13.

Etztak was seized by a terrible rage. He stamped the floor with his feet and shouted at his officers although there was not one man in the command centre who could be held responsible for the misfortune.

His observers had already located a minute and a half ago the craft which had so suddenly appeared – and the disturbance caused by the transition of the adversary was registered at the same moment it occurred.

However that report never reached Etztak's ears. He raved on and on and was completely unaware that he himself was the sole reason that denied final success to the ETZ XXI.

'Commander to fire-control officers! We have no intention of destroying the enemy. All we want to do is to get him off the back of the Z-13. Be prepared for a sudden return by transition!' The crew was alerted.

The *Solar System* raced to meet the hostile battleship with maximum acceleration. The distance shrunk rapidly and the velocity of the Terranian ship increased by the second.

'Ten more seconds to reach firing range!' the Second Officer announced.

'Fire within range!' Nyssen commanded tersely.

The 10 seconds seemed to be endless. Nyssen watched them tick slowly by on the chronometer, cursing his lameness.

Still five seconds to go!

What was the range of the enemy's guns?

Nyssen had no knowledge of the events taking place on the ETZ XXI which had brought on Etztak's horrendous wrath. But he saw the disintegrator beams and the white-blue energy rays shoot through space as the little Z-13 dodged madly.

Nyssen estimated the range of the energy rays by their luminosity. Calculating roughly with lightning speed he determined that it was comparable to his own cannons. No later than his own rayguns reached the enemy, the foe could hit the *Solar System* too.

One more second!

The green lamp started blinking at the same moment the alarm commenced wailing.

The *Solar System* had begun to fight!

'Where is the enemy ship?' Etztak fumed.

The rangefinder officer cited the coordinates with the last bit of self-restraint he could muster. Etztak glanced at the screen to see the picture of the foe.

Even before he recognized it, he waved to the fire-control officer. The officer passed the order on—'Focus on new target with rangefinder data!'

Simultaneously Etztak saw the opponent. Not directly but the faint green bundle of rays which broke loose from a point in space and two seconds later filled the entire picture screen.

A jolt of unbelievable force jarred the ETZ XXI. The brilliant light disappeared and was replaced by the dim glow of the emergency lamps.

Alarm whistles shrilled and a din of voices came out of the loudspeakers.

Etztak was thrown to the floor. In spite of the tumult reigning in the command centre one of his aides did his duty and rushed immediately to his assistance. He helped him to get back on his feet again. Etztak regained his self-control in a remarkably short time.

'Hit?' he asked curtly.

'Yes, Sire!' the man replied. 'In the engine room.'

Etztak stroked his forehead. His towering rage had left him. For a few seconds he was a helpless old man.

Then he called the engine room. He was told that two important aggregates had been knocked out and that the ETZ XXI was still operable although its performance was reduced to 60%.

Etztak gave orders to break off the pursuit and turn around.

The rangefinder reported that the large ship had disappeared.

The little speck kept racing through the universe. During the seconds after the hit when the ETZ XXI had continued its forward motion without speeding up further, the little machine accelerated again and went beyond the limit where the cannons of the huge ship were lethal.

'Let him go,' Etztak growled. 'Perhaps the battle fleet will get him. We'll return and join the others again. Pass on the order to the WENA and HORL.'

For a fraction of a second Nyssen toyed with the idea

of taking the Z-13 on board and jumping back together. However the operation would have taken under the best of circumstances at least half a minute and Nyssen considered it too risky to remain another half a minute under the guns of the enemy.

Therefore Bell received the laconic message from the *Solar System*: 'Daisy must take care of herself again!'

Then the *Solar System* disappeared from this sector of space.

Bell felt disappointed and relieved at the same time. He braked his speed as hard as he could and pulled the Z-13 around in a tight curve on his new course. The destroyer was carried past the Springer fleet at a distance of a few light-seconds, far enough to be safe.

The warships didn't seem to have any intention of following him. Either Nyssen's success in disabling Etztak's formidable vessel had made them cautious or they simply figured they had come here for other purposes.

Bell didn't try very long to find the explanation although he had plenty of time. After he changed his course by 180° he increased his speed to the extreme. But the *Stardust* was eight light-hours away and even with the relative shortening of time he would still require more than half a Terra-day to reach security again.

CHAPTER TWO

PSYCHO-GRILL

On the ice planet – which they had given the name Snowman – nothing was noticed of the events that had occurred in outer space. Aubrey's capacity for observation was limited. He had been unable to spot Etztak's tremendous spaceship because it was too far from him above the Snowman surface and the cadets were unaware of the chase after the Z-13.

The deceptive calm made the cadets nervous. They had realized that their presence on Snowman was required by Perry Rhodan for a definite purpose because he could have picked them up and saved them many times already. This was ample proof of his motives and they were now convinced that the whole uproar the Springers caused was indeed because of them.

Tiff was at the mercy of Hifield who raked him over the coals.

'Now that you got us into this mess,' Hifield pestered 'the least you can do is tell us what Rhodan has in mind for us.'

Tiff had told Hifield ten times already during recent hours that he knew as little about Rhodan's plan as anybody else. From the eleventh time on he simply refused to take notice of Hifield's reproaches.

Periodically Tiff went over to the ravine to listen in on the automatic recording equipment of the patrol craft. Shortly after they had settled down in their cave, Rhodan had informed them by this method that they had to hold out for a while longer and had promised them support. Since that short message, however, no other word had been transmitted.

Tiff had hoped to be able to use the hypercom set to monitor the communications among the Springers. Unfortunately this was frustrated by the Springers who had immediately changed the frequency as a consequence of the loss of the patrolship.

The way from the cave to the little machine was rather difficult, at some places even downright dangerous on slippery ice. However, the low gravity of Snowman favoured the climber.

On his way back to the shelter Tiff wrestled in his quandry with a decision whether or not to induce his people to move farther south – out of the zone of danger. Of course, during hours of marching they would be helplessly exposed to the rangefinders of the enemy. But the instruments of their pursuers would not cover every square inch of the ice planet's surface. If they were lucky . . .

Should a strategist make plans trusting to luck? Tiff mused and laughed at himself for using the term 'strategist'. It seemed that his laugh was audible through the helmet radio in the cave. Mildred's mild voice asked: 'What's so funny?'

Tiff answered in amusement: 'Oh nothing, really!'

He was still about 100 feet away from the cave. On

second thought he felt that Mildred's friendly question deserved a better answer. He began: 'You know . . .'

And then he hit the ground. He did it instinctively. There was not enough time for his brain to react sensibly to the black bales suddenly dropping from the sky. Tiff heard a whooshing sound in the outside mike and a dull thud as the dark objects landed on the ice. Simultaneously he heard a shrill whistle.

He pulled up the thermo-beamer he had taken away from the Springer and cautiously peered out of the snow at the strange bundles.

Bombs! was the first thought flashing through his mind. Yet the objects didn't look like bombs.

Tiff slowly got up and approached the packages with drawn weapon. 'Stay inside!' he warned. 'Something fell down from the sky.'

Mildred and Felicita cried in fright: 'For heaven's sake, Tiff! Watch yourself!' And Eberhardt called: 'Are you sure you don't want me to come out?'

'Quite sure,' Tiff replied.

He stood only 20 feet from the first package when he discovered the figure. Tiff planted his feet firmly in the snow and trained his weapon on the form. He stared with incredulous eyes at the three-foot-long figure clad in a special spacesuit, that was lying yards away in the snow. Slowly he lowered his weapon and put it back in his pocket.

'Pucky!' he gasped. 'I mean, sir . . .'

'Oh be quiet!' Pucky ordered. 'I took a stupendous spill.'

The mouse-beaver raised himself up and hobbled over to Tiff, moving much slower than usual.

Tiff saluted and stood at attention. Pucky, being a mutant of the highest order, held the rank of an officer. It might have looked ludicrous but Pucky had to be shown the proper respect of his rank.

Tiff's face began to light up. 'It's great that you came to see us, sir! Nonetheless you've given us quite a scare.'

'I regret that I was unable to announce my arrival,' Pucky replied and his eyes sparkled mockingly through the faceplate of his space helmet.

'Of course not, sir!' Tiff admitted. 'May I show you our hide-away?'

Tiff showed the way and opened the cover plate of the first partition protecting the inner recess of the cave against the forbidding cold of Snowman. A surge of warm air escaped and turned immediately to a fine fog in the cold.

Pucky followed Tiff. He watched with a practised eye how Tiff replaced the plate fashioned from molten metal and removed the closure of the second wall. 'Good job!' he praised him.

One by one they passed through six separating walls until they reached the living quarters behind the last partition which were adequately shielded from the cold and kept warm by Aubrey's thermobeamer switched on low.

Pucky allowed that he had not expected to find so much comfort and commended them for their efficiency. Finally he said in a formal language he seemed to enjoy: 'I herewith deliver a consignment of energy weapons, Arkonide transport-suits, additional provisions and equipment which you'll find useful.'

'Where?' Eberhardt asked in a baffled tone.

Tiff pointed back over his shoulder to the outside. 'In the packages Pucky has brought along with him.'

Etztak ordered his ship to land. It had been determined that the damage from the enemy's shot was comparatively easy and quick to repair once the maintenance crew was on solid ground.

Shortly after they had touched down Etztak requested the Springer Orlgans, Captain of ORLA XI, to come on board.

Etztak made a *request*, although he had supreme authority over the entire clan in a time of crisis like this, because he considered it more sensible to retain conventional manners as long as it was possible and useful.

The Springers were a peculiar people related to the Arkonides. The Arkonides had created a Galactic Imperium around their home world Arkon, building it up to a zenith of power and then sliding into a state of decadence. The Springers, however, had separated themselves very early from the original race and established a way of life of their own. They became traders. A claim to be the only people entitled to conduct interstellar trade was related to the ancient mythical beginning of their history. They never were a unified nation. Each captain, member of a special caste, owned his ship and took care of his exclusive trade and to snatch a deal away from another Springer was the most precious pleasure he could imagine.

Nevertheless they all felt a kinship and the universe considered them as a distinct group. They had managed to amass such a wealth of experience and to make themselves so useful and indispensable in the Arkonide Imperium that nobody else carried on any trade worth mentioning.

They had frequently run into belligerent resistance and had built an armada of warships with the fortune they had gained. The Springers benefited from the experiences of the Arkonide technology and from those of other races they came in contact with. Even at this time when the events on Snowman took place nobody really knew who was the more dominant power, the Springers or the Arkonides.

Although the Springers doubtlessly contributed to the slow decay of the Imperium, there had never been a direct confrontation between them and the Arkonides. The Springers did their most lucrative trade by remaining neutral and selling weapons to both parties in a conflict.

There was no place the Springers could call home as they never settled in any one world of the Galaxy. Their ships were designed to land only in emergencies. They lived on their vessels in free space and sprang from system to system to carry on their business.

That was why they called themselves Springers.

Each member was entitled to the protection by their battle fleet. All he had to do in case of need, was to call for help and it would arrive on the spot in the shortest time.

This is what had happened to Captain Orlgans and his ship ORLA XI. He had by accident come upon some merchant ships engaged in the exchange of goods between the planet Ferrol in the Vega system and the Earth in system Sol. The commerce was the result of a treaty Perry Rhodan had signed on his trip to Ferrol with the government of the Thort.

Orlgans suspected a violation of the trade monopoly of his race. Since he also smelled a profit he wanted to handle the matter by himself. He landed on Venus and sent special agents to Earth. Orlgans succeeded in capturing a ship of the Terranian space fleet, took its crew prisoners and transported them together with their ship to a safe place.

The captain learned from his agents that an important person of the Terranian space fleet was due to leave the Earth in another spaceship in a short time. The man, they said, was informed about the World of Eternal Life – that mysterious planet recounted in age-old legends whose existence was believed by all.

Orlgans coveted this information. He was anxious to obtain it at all costs as it would lead to the most important deal of his life. He ambushed the ship on which the man in question had embarked and fettered it with magneto-mechanical bonds to his own vessel. Then he jumped through hyperspace into the Beta–Albireo system to get as far away as possible from the inimical environment of Terra.

Orlgans had interrogated his man – the Cadet

Julian Tifflor – several times but Tifflor steadfastly maintained that he didn't have the desired information.

Soon thereafter a task force of three mammoth ships of the Terranian fleet arrived on the scene in the Beta–Albireo sector. Orlgans called for help and received it at once – 30 units of the Springer armada. In the ensuing fracas Tifflor's little ship, captured by Orlgans, managed to escape. The ship itself had been taken aboard by one of the immense Terrestrial ships after Tifflor had fled in a tiny destroyer. Eventually he crash-landed on Snowman, having suffered severe damage from a Springer battleship.

The victorious Terranian fighting team had forced the Springer group to retreat while the ORLA XI kept on the side lines and sneaked away from the imbroglio.

Orlgans had noticed Tifflor's plight and his emergency landing on the ice planet. After the battle was over he returned and resumed his search for Tifflor. He discovered his tracks and found out that the cadet was not alone. Orlgans dispatched a patrol craft after the fugitives. The cadets tricked the two-man crew into surrender, seized their vessel and released their two pursuers again.

The sudden appearance of the armada of 90 ships was not entirely welcome to Orlgans. Of course he had expected the war fleet to return with reinforcements after they had been dealt such a humiliating setback but he had not the slightest intention of letting all the rival Springer captains in on his business on Snowman and all the involved implications.

Orlgans obediently followed Etztak's invitation and flew in an auxiliary ship over the ETZ XXI. Men from the repair crew were stuck like little flies on the outer skin close to the place where the disintegrator shot from the Terranian battleship had gouged a hole in the huge body.

The visitor entered the ship through the airlock, glided up the shaft of the antigrav elevator and stepped from the door of the shaft on to a conveyor running the entire length of the main corridor.

Only 20 minutes after Etztak had voiced his demand Orlgans stood before the patriarch greeting him with respect and in a formal manner.

Etztak was not a man to waste his time on preliminary niceties although he had seen Orlgans during the past 15 years only on a hypercom screen. 'We've got to finish this matter right away,' Etztak said bluntly; '90 warships are lying in wait out there. We're sunk if one of the captains gets wind of our enterprise!'

'How could they find out lest we have a traitor in our clan?' Orlgans queried.

Etztak disregarded the remark. 'Never mind what devious ways they can use. The longer it takes us to get to the bottom of this, the more risk we'll have to run. I've studied your report carefully. You believe this stranger can divulge information about the location of the World of Eternal Life, don't you?'

'Yes,' Orlgans replied.

'How did you find that out?' Etztak wanted to know.

'By accident,' Orlgans explained. Then he proceeded to tell once more the whole story which he had already mentioned in his written report. The story of the prisoner he had made and of the disturbances caused by the transition in the Vega system.

Orlgans was familiar with the patriarch's method. By comparison of the oral with the written report he tried to learn whether a captain of his clan had tried to keep something from him.

'Good,' Etztak finally grunted. 'What kind of a man is your prisoner?'

'He's an avowed enemy of the man who plays the most important role on the strange planet. We picked him up when he fled from that man.'

'What's his name?'

Orlgans had already stated it in his report. However he deferentially answered Etztak's question: 'Mouselet.'

Etztak furrowed his brow. 'What does he know?'

'Not much. He knows the organization and names of our enemies. But he never heard of the World of Eternal Life.'

'So he says!'

Orlgans looked up. 'I've not yet put him through a psycho-grill because he may not survive it. But I don't believe that he lied to me.'

'Let's bring in the man! We'll dig out of him what he knows. We don't have time left to pussyfoot around with a stranger.'

Orlgans raised no objections. He called the ORLA XI from Etztak's flagship and gave instructions to have three men escort the prisoner to the ETZ XXI as quickly as possible.

Jean-Pierre Mouselet had been incarcerated in one of the rooms of the ORLA XI ever since his capture a few months ago. He belonged to the retinue of the infamous and powerful Supermutant who had striven to destroy Rhodan and set himself up as ruler of the Earth and eventually of the whole universe.

Mouselet cursed the day when he set foot on board the ORLA XI and in retrospect, being consistent, also the hour when he was pressed into the service of the Supermutant. Admittedly the Supermutant hadn't had to exert too much pressure in his case since Mouselet was rather eager to work for him, hoping to make a lot of money. In the last ship the Supermutant had left, Mouselet slipped away from Terra. At the last moment before his nemesis caught up with him, he discovered the alien spaceship, accosted it and asked for permission to board.

And there he was. He wished he had never—

The hatch of the small room was opened without warning. Mouselet jumped up from his chair. A tall, stubble-bearded Springer stood in the door frame, his thermo-weapon pointed at the Frenchman in an unmistakable threat.

The guard said something unintelligible and two seconds later the little set he had pinned below his neck intoned his order clearly in French: 'Come with me!'

Mouselet's eyes lit up. He rushed forward without paying attention to the weapon in the Springer's hand and stammered: 'Have you got . . . a cigaret . . . for me?'

He stood still and waited, trembling, till the little

instrument translated his question into the alien language. The Springer frowned and answered something which was later translated: 'What's . . . a cigaret?'

Mouselet's shoulders drooped again. He had asked the question so often and always received the same reply. He no longer believed that he would ever smoke another cigaret – unless they sent him back to Earth.

He stepped through the hatch with lowered head and the guard showed him the way through the corridors.

They shoved him roughly into a room where two men were seated, one of whom he knew. Two of the three guards who had accompanied Mouselet remained outside in the corridor but the man with the translator came in with him.

'What do you know about the World of Eternal Life?' Etztak asked brusquely and the little set translated the question.

Mouselet looked up in surprise. With a mixture of fright and astonishment he gazed at the imposing white-haired patriarch. Then he glanced with a pleading look in his eyes at Orlgans whom he knew. But Orlgans' face was stern and immobile.

'I don't . . . I don't know . . . what you're talking about,' Mouselet stammered and the translator repeated his answer with the same stammer.

Etztak stood up abruptly and the sight of the broad-shouldered giant startled and intimidated Mouselet even more

'Psycho-interrogation,' Etztak stipulated and the translation followed.

Mouselet had no idea what a psycho-interrogation was but the word itself was enough to scare him to death. He begn to protest. 'Please, listen to me!' he whimpered and the mechanical voice of the translator trailing a few words behind increased his terror. 'I'm willing to tell you all I know but I've never heard of a World of Eternal Life. What's it supposed to be? A planet? Or perhaps a country on some planet?'

The two Springers looked silently at each other. Finally Etztak raised his hand and waved to the guard. Mouselet understood the ominous sign.

'No!' he screamed. 'Please, no psycho-interrogation! I can tell you no more than I did already.'

The guard grabbed the puny Frenchman and dragged him out into the corridor and to the interrogation chamber 600 feet away.

'I really don't believe he knows anything.' Orlgans expressed the doubt in his mind.

Etztak admitted grudgingly: 'Maybe so. Perhaps he knows something subconsciously relating to the World of Eternal Life. The only dependable way of obtaining a systematic review of his memory content is by subjecting him to the psycho-grill. The analyser doesn't forget any information.'

'But the man will be destroyed in the process,' Orlgans voiced his misgivings.

'What do you care?' Etztak challenged him with a disdainful gesture.

'I didn't come here to do all your work,' Pucky protested. 'However I intend to investigate the situation thoroughly myself. We simply must know where the enemy can be ferreted out. As soon as we have found that out it'll be up to each one of us to make short shrift of them. I want to brief you on our objectives. The Springers have already made it clear that they're interested in Terra. According to the information we've so far collected their interest is of a hostile nature. Since the Springers are a technologically highly advanced race it is vital that we prepare ourselves for the coming confrontation to the best of our ability. For this purpose it is essential to gather intelligence and this is precisely our task on Snowman. We need to know what the Springers have up their sleeves and what measures they plan to take to advance their goal. It is imperative that we find out who their agents on Earth are and why we haven't been able to trace them down. Once we've ascertained all this, our mission will be finished here.'

He winked at Tiff, changing in a jiffy from an officer of the Mutant Corps into the droll furball they all knew. 'You probably know by now,' he addressed Tiff, 'what kind of a game Rhodan played with you during the past days. Rhodan has sent you out as a man with allegedly important information. Apparently the trick was successful, seeing how the Springers fell for it.'

He didn't give Tiff time to recover from the awful surprise. He assigned jobs to the three cadets and instructed the girls in their tasks. Then he asked Aubrey to give him the coördinates of the closest enemy ship and disappeared in a teleportation jump after fixing a time for his return.

Mouselet's examination lasted only a few minutes. The machine probing him operated rapidly, precisely and unfeelingly. When Mouselet was released from the chair where he sat during the procedure, he had ceased to be an intelligent creature.

It was the function of the analyser to scour the brain of the tested person, store the data and furnish it at the termination. It operated with such exhaustive intensity that all it left was a squeezed out mass of brain which was barely capable of regulating the animal activities of a man.

Holloran, the guard, loaded Mouselet, who was Mouselet no longer, into a patrol craft and flew him back to the ORLA XI. Mouselet offered no resistance. Holloran took him to his room and locked him up.

Then he started out again to take the auxiliary ship back to the ETZ XXI and to ask Orlgans what he wanted him to do next.

The ORLA XI had been grounded at the beginning of the action because Orglans had considered it necessary to occupy a fixed position. The ship was stationed about six miles from the ETZ XXI.

Holloran had just left the airlock of the ORLA XI when his little craft began to lose speed and altitude and failed to respond to his steering controls. The vessel acted as if it were sucked downwards and its engine had become faulty. He had been flying fairly close to the ground. Before he could check his instruments or send an emergency signal to one of the other ships, his machine touched the fluffy white mass and slowed down to a stop leaving a swirling scintillating trail of snow behind. Holloran held on tightly to the control panel but this proved to be unnecessary. The landing was smooth and neither the pilot nor the vessel were hurt.

The Springer was completely vexed as he looked around. The vessel was half buried in the snow. The panoramic observation screen barely showed the upper outline of the ORLA XI as a grey line in the west. Nothing could be seen of the ETZ XXI from his low position.

Holloran studied his dials and the longer he looked the more baffled he was. Everything seemed to be in working condition including the engine. Why did the vehicle go down?

With knit brow Holloran tired to start up again. He only had to move the vertical lift one step and . . .

Nothing! It was impossible to shift the lever. Incredulously Holloran tried harder, to no avail. Finally he pounded on the lever with his fist but all was in vain: the lever still refused to budge.

Holloran sat still a few seconds in stupefaction. Then he realized that there was nothing left to do but to send a call for help to the ORLA XI to come and get him and his ship. Mechanically he reached for the transmitter switch and tried to press it. He was severely consternated when he noticed that he was unable to move the switch. Holloran tested other switches at random. They worked properly. He turned the emergency light on and off, as well as the climate control, the sensors and the picture screen.

But he didn't need the emergency light nor the climate control, sensor and screen, what he needed was the vertical lift and the transmitter. Holloran looked around to see if there might be another ship going by in the neighbourhood which could detect him by accident. But the sky was empty as far as he could see.

He began to worry about his predicament. Without luck he could be stranded helplessly in the snow for days, unable to leave his ship since he didn't wear a spacesuit. He had only intended to fly from one airlock to the other, for which he didn't require the protection of a spacesuit. They wouldn't miss him very soon. He was only an ordinary member of the crew and not a very important personality.

And if nobody missed him at all and he was not picked up by pure chance . . .

In the middle of the thought Holloran's mind ceased to function. He believed he heard a soft mocking laugh and a voice telling him: 'Don't you fret, son! I'll be right back and then we'll fly away again.'

A long time before Reginald Bell returned with the Z-13 the highly sensitive telepath John Marshall on board the *Stardust* received a mental message from Pucky that his arrival on the ice planet and the transfer of the equipment had proceeded without a hitch. Pucky added that he first wanted to reconnoitre the positions of the enemy before he started with the specific task of gathering the desired information.

Marshall gave the message to Rhodan. Having only meagre knowledge of Rhodan's plans, he was surprised to see that a big load seemed to be lifted off Rhodan's mind when he heard about Pucky's success.

After Marshall had left the *Stardust*'s spacious command centre where only Rhodan and Khrest were present at the time, Rhodan said: 'I'm happy that everything went fine. The venture is terribly risky for Tifflor and his four people. They might easily have been lost if Pucky had failed to do his job right.'

Khrest the Arkonide looked at him thoughtfully. 'I've been wondering all the time how, shall we say, frivolously you've used these people.'

Rhodan smiled. He understood Khrest and his way of thinking. The Arkonide leader of an explorative expedition whose vessel was shipwrecked on Luna, belonged to a culture whose peak had already been passed at the time mankind entered the Stone Age. It was a characteristic of the Arkonide philosophy after the Imperium had reached the apex of its power and had stopped further development that the life of an individual was valued so highly that it should not be sacrificed by society even if the nation was in distress. A principle, Rhodan thought, only a satiated society could afford.

'You know,' Rhodan answered, still smiling, 'I don't believe you'll ever understand this. Nevertheless, I firmly believe I've done the right thing, even though Tifflor's chances were only 50-50 at the outset.'

Khrest turned his attention to the instruments again which he had offered to monitor. The sensors registered no irregularities. The two hostile fleets performed no transitions, if they moved at all. Quiet reigned in the Beta–Albireo sector.

The lull before a storm.

Holloran was not yet over his first shock when he was hit by a second which was even worse.

Suddenly a creature sat beside him as if it had always been there. He had never seen its like before. At first glance he would have thought it an animal except for the fact that it was clad in a spacesuit.

The creature was only half as big as Holloran. It had a pointed snout, large ears and a plump rear end. The eyes were big and looked through the faceplate at Holloran with amused blinking.

Suddenly Holloran heard the voice again: 'I don't mind if you take a *little* time gaping at me but don't dally too long. I'm in a hurry!'

Holloran was completely shaken up. *A telepath,* he thought. *He seems to know a few other tricks too. Perhaps it's his fault that the switches are stuck.*

'You only have to think what you want to tell me,' Holloran was informed. 'If you don't like it you may talk to me. I'll understand you.'

The Springer shuddered. A being who could read each of his thoughts. 'What do you want?' he asked perplexed.

'Not much,' came the answer. 'I would like to get into that big ship over there. Since they won't let me in willingly, you'll have to sneak me in with your craft.'

'Impossible!' Holloran panted. 'They'd kill me if they found out I did it.'

'So much the better for me,' was the reply. 'That way you'll keep your mouth shut and mention me to nobody.'

Holloran continued to protest but the furry creature produced a raygun from a pocket and pointed it at the Springer, holding it in his forepaw which was enclosed in the thin skin of the protective suit.

'Get going now!' Holloran heard. 'And cut out the gab!'

Holloran realized that he had no other choice than to follow his orders. Slowly and suspiciously his hand reached the level for the vertical lift. Hesitantly and cautiously he pushed and . . .

Click! The lever slid smoothly and the engine began to hum. Then he stepped the control up and the little machine responded perfectly, rising above the snow.

'Very good!' Pucky lauded him. 'Keep going. Do they control admittance to the big ship?'

Holloran was puzzled by the question. 'Yes . . . of course,' he answered in a quivering voice.

Again he heard the derisive laugh by which the strange being had made himself first noticeable. 'It's no use lying to me. As I told you, I can read your thoughts. Well, then there are no controls. That's better. We won't have any difficulties.'

Holloran swore silently. It was his rotten luck to get into such an unpleasant predicament.

In the east the ETZ XXI came into view above the snow. Holloran glanced to the side. The furry being seemed to pay no attention to him but the gun was still in his hand. Holloran had no way out. He was forced to do as he was told.

The matter was deemed to be so important that Orlgans and Etztak took over the job of studying the evaluation. The analyser had produced a total of 24 diagrams relating to Mouselet's interrogation – one for each relevant section of his brain. The coördinates of the calibrated points – each diagram contained between 1000 and 10,000 such measurements – together with the weighted significance of the biological-statistical data, were fed into a mechanical evaluator. This machine delivered the decoded information in concise key-words printed on small plastic strips.

After half an hour it had become perfectly obvious that Jean-Pierre Mouselet indeed knew nothing at all about the World of Eternal Life. Etztak was so disgusted that he threw another fit of temper. He was about to sweep the plastic strips from the table when Orlgans stayed his hand and shouted: 'Look here! This is a clue!'

Etztak had trouble calming down. Angrily he tore the strip from Orlgans' hand and held it before his eyes. 'It is clear,' Orlgans murmured, 'that Terra has no inkling of the Springers' scheme. If Rhodan is going to take a hand in this matter his first step will be to secure information.'

'So what?' Etztak growled. 'That's trivial!'

Orlgans handed him a second strip. It bore a marginal note by the analyser: Basic attitude – caustic.

'If I know Rhodan,' Etztak continued reading,

'he'll place a spy so close in front of the Springers' nose that they won't be able to see him with their big eyes and Tifflor would be just the man to do the job.' Etztak jumped out of his skin. 'That . . . that!' he panted.

Orlgans' face had a doubtful expression. 'That doesn't necessarily mean,' he interrupted the old man, 'that we're on the wrong track. The prisoner doesn't know anything about the World of Eternal Life and consequently cannot know whether Tifflor is acquainted with it or not. But his impression seems important to me anyway.'

'I should say it is!' Etztak roared, pounding the table with his fist. 'It's always important to know the mentality of your enemy. The prisoner knew Rhodan better than we do. If he thinks that's how Rhodan operates, then he's probably right. One thing I'd like to know though. How does it come that the prisoner knows that person by the name of Tifflor?'

Orlgans rummaged through the information strips and picked up three more of them. The strips pertained to the fact that Mouselet had some dealings with Tifflor during his activities ordered by the Supermutant. It was some disagreeable encounter but the hardened Mouselet had come away with a feeling of respect for Tifflor.

Etztak was satisfied. He looked with flashing eyes at Orlgans who could sense a new wave of vigour and resolve flowing from the old man.

'If that is the case,' Etztak's strong voice thundered, accompanying his words with a resounding laugh, 'then we've no longer any reason to sit here idly. We'll have to start a minute search of the vicinity of our landing place.'

Orlgans agreed. 'I'd suggest,' he added, however, 'including the neighbourhood of the place where the fugitives seized the patrol craft of the ORLA XI.'

'We'll do that too,' Etztak assented.

Preparations for the search were made at once. Etztak applied a lesson he had learned from Orlgans' experience. As a result he instructed the search teams not to leave their vehicles under any circumstances. Furthermore, at least two ships had to remain in sight of each other at all times while patrolling the area.

'If the prisoner was right,' Etztak's voice reverberated from the intercom, 'it shouldn't take more than a few hours to catch the fugitives.'

CHAPTER THREE

DEATH ON SNOWMAN

Holloran's auxiliary ship shot with remarkable speed into the dark gaping hole of the large hangar airlock.

Pucky perceived from Holloran's thoughts that the Springer was not inclined to end his own life or that of his intruding guest. He strictly proceeded in the usual manner. The little machine braked quickly but gently and floated through a passage leading to the individual pads of the patrol ships. From a certain point on the vehicle seemed to be conducted automatically. Holloran had stopped manipulating his controls but a few moments later the ship was firmly secured on the pad by a stationary gravitational field.

'Here we are,' Holloran stated.

Pucky thanked him ironically. He remained for a moment motionlessly in his seat and deduced from Holloran's mind the layout of the huge ship, at least in rough outlines. Of the information culled involuntarily from the Springer, Pucky selected one piece in particular for his use. It concerned a spare parts stockroom in the rear section of the ETZ XXI which Holloran knew to be empty and practically never used.

Just as Holloran was about to leave the ship and wanted to ask his guest about his further wishes, Pucky departed. Holloran stared in frightened disbelief at the seat where the furry animal had sat. He broke out in perspiration thinking about the havoc which could be wrought by such a being on the ship and felt even more miserable when he remembered that – in order to save his own skin – he was unable to tell anybody what kind of a strange stowaway he had brought aboard.

Pale and trembling he climbed out and went to the nearest intercom set and reported to the hangar control officer that he had returned and duly berthed the patrol ship.

Pucky materialized again safely and without complications in the little stockroom. He noticed at once that Holloran's information was either false or old since the walls of the room were covered with cabinets and each compartment was filled to overflowing. The room was not as quiet and remote as Pucky had expected. But at least for the time being there were no Springers present.

With the probing sense which was part of his telekinetic ability he carefully checked the immediate surroundings of the stockroom. Up to a distance of 15 feet he was able to feel the outline of objects which were out of his sight. As cautious as he was, he didn't take the time to identify the outlines of what was outside. It was enough for him to know nothing within 15 feet of him was moving.

When he was certain he jumped out. He landed in

front of the stockroom hatch in a narrow winding gangway which ended a few feet behind him at a flat shiny wall. Pucky mind-probed through the wall and felt icy gusts of snow beyond the outer hull of the ship. He had to turn in the opposite direction to find out what he had come for. He ambled down the narrow gangway which twisted at sharp corners every 10 to 12 feet, reaching with his 'feelers' around the next corner. In this manner he avoided the danger that he might accidentally run into somebody.

After the tenth bend the narrow gangway ended in a much larger corridor which, to his chagrin, ran straight. Pucky tip-toed forward and probed the corridor, finding it deserted as far as he could sense. When he finally looked around into the corridor which was lit much brighter than the gangway, he saw that it was empty only 60 feet in both directions. He noticed many figures rushing through the corridor and disappearing in the recesses of the wall where apparently the antigrav elevators were located.

Pucky counted 30 Springers on each side. He waited till all the Springers had entered the elevators. Then he teleported himself as far as he could see down the corridor. He appeared again at a crossing of another passageway which ended at the left in another wider corridor whose floor was equipped with conveyor walk belts in both directions. He recognized that he had reached the main hallway of the ship. If he judged the Springers correctly, the command centre should be situated somewhere along this hallway and probably right in the middle.

The commander was the man Pucky wanted to

meet as the most likely source of the desired information. Therefore he had to advance along the hallway until he found the command centre unknown to him.

And that, Pucky decided, was ticklish and far from easy but it had to be done nevertheless.

'Foreign objects!' Aubrey announced briefly.

Tiff looked up. 'What is it, Aubrey?' he asked.

'A great number of small ships, sir!' Aubrey replied. 'In many different places. Together in pairs. The nearest at R 50,000, Phi 5. Altitude constant at 1000 feet.'

Tiff got up. 'So they're still after us,' he said gravely. 'Let's get ready!'

Hifield didn't budge. He leaned his strong back against the wall and eyed Tiff suspiciously. 'How do you know it's the Springers?' he asked disgruntled.

'Sure, you're right. They're probably Eskimos.' Tiff dismissed it, paying no further attention to Hifield.

The packages Pucky had brought had been hauled in and unpacked long ago. The Arkonide transport suits were neatly spread out in the background and ready to slip in.

Tiff took off his spacesuit and put on the transport suit. Eberhardt followed his example while Hifield was still sitting motionlessly with his back against the wall.

Eberhardt taunted him: 'Are you afraid of the Springers, Hifield?'

Hifield rose up and angrily threatened Eberhardt:

'Don't say that again!' Then he too started to change into a transportation suit.

'Control check!' Tiff ordered. 'Deflector field?'

'O.K.'

'Impact screen?'

'O.K.'

'Antigrav?'

'O.K.'

'Climate control?'

'O.K.'

'Very good!'

Tiff turned to the girls. 'You stay here and don't move!' he advised them.

Then he went to Aubrey and instructed him. 'Take up your position at the outer partition. Don't expose yourself outside the cave unless I call you. It's too easy for them to locate a hunk of metal like you.'

'Will do, sir!' Aubrey confirmed.

Tiff looked around once more. 'I wish Pucky were already back,' he murmured, adding in a loud voice: 'Close your helmets! Take your arms! Use minimum of energy for helmet transmitters!'

They complied and Tiff said: 'Now let's get going!'

Aubrey removed the cover from the wall. A draft of cold air came in. The robot squeezed through the narrow opening. Tiff followed him with Eberhardt and Hifield behind.

'Distance now 15,000 feet, sir!' Aubrey reported as he replaced the cover. 'Phi unchanged, altitude remains at 1000 feet.'

Tiff understood. *Phi unchanged* meant that the two

ships were closing in on the centre of the coördinate system. And the centre was Tiff with his cell transmitter.

'Seems to me that we've a fair-sized mountain in front of us,' Willagar said.

And Psholgur added: 'I'd think if somebody wanted to hide from us he'd do it in a mountainous region rather than dig in on the plain.'

Willagar laughed. 'That makes two of us then with the same opinion.'

Willagar and Psholgur were the crew of one of the two patrol craft Aubrey had spotted. Willagar contacted the second ship over the telecom and told its occupants about their mutual suspicions.

Horlgon – a young member of the Horl family who owned the HORL VII – and Enaret thought that this suspicion was well-founded too. 'Then we better watch out from now on,' Horlgon warned. 'We're about 250 miles from the spot where the fugitives seized the ship. They could very well have hidden in this area.'

'That's exactly what I believe,' Willagar answered. Let's slow down our speed as soon as we reach the mountains.'

'All right,' Horlgon agreed.

Tiff had to suppress a touch of homesickness when he looked at his watch. 6.51 o'clock Terrestrial time. A new morning dawned on Earth at this time.

Here on Snowman the shining point of light, the blue-white sun, neared the horizon and even though the orange-coloured disc of the central sun would remain in the sky, it was too weak after the blue-white dwarf went down to give more light than a fair moon.

They stationed themselves at the rim of the ravine where the patrol craft was hidden. Tiff was in constant contact with Aubrey who waited behind the first wall in the cave monitoring the position of the two ships. Tiff had realized for some time that his pursuers concentrated their search on the mountains where their cave was located. They had changed their course and flew in ever tighter circles around a spot only a few miles away from the cave.

Willagar and Psholgur tried out a new method. They held their ship at an altitude of about 300 feet and rotated the beam of their sensor. Horlgon and Enaret stayed within sight as ordered by Etztak. None of the four expected they would be able to locate the fugitives since they probably had crawled into a cave long ago. But they figured they had a good chance of spotting the captured patrol ship if the sensor were given an opportunity to work accurately.

It was Horlgon who detected the lost ship. He determined the coördinates and Willagar too directed his sensor beam at the described place.

'We want to take up another position,' suggested Willagar.

Horlgon's voice sounded very excited as he replied: 'Okay. We don't want them to notice that we've discovered them in case they've already made us out.'

It annoyed Willager that Horlgon was wise to his tactic.

Tiff's observations were very simple and convincing. 'Since two hours,' he explained, 'they have used a new system. They hover for 20 minutes over a spot and comb the surroundings as far as their instruments reach. They've done this already five times. The sixth time, when they were almost vertically above the ravine, they moved away after eight minutes. If that doesn't mean they've detected the ship and left as a ruse for us, you can call me a fool.'

'All right, fool!' Hifield reacted. 'I think you're too pessimistic.'

Tiff didn't have to answer. Eberhardt intervened: 'It seems perfectly clear to me. I'd have done the same thing, perhaps a little less obvious though.'

Aubrey reported the latest positions. The two ships had now approached within 1000 feet beyond the cave.

'Let's wait and see!' Tiff proposed. 'If they've found the ship they're bound to change their strategy sooner or later.'

Eberhardt grunted. 'I'd like to be able to see you again. Is the deflector really necessary?'

'We must keep using it,' Tiff replied firmly. 'We don't know the range of their instruments.'

Pucky waited about half an hour at the junction of the side corridor. He deftly evaded all those in whose brains he could perceive from a safe distance that it would be impossible to proceed unseen to the commander by the direct way. What he needed was more precise information about the location of the room which the commander occupied. Pucky moved farther back into the little used side corridor and picked a spot from where he could easily jump into an adjacent room in case a group of Springers passed by. Then he waited.

In the first 10 minutes nobody came his way and there was no need for him to take a jump. Shortly thereafter a bunch of Springers hurried through the gangway but their thoughts were too helter-skelter for Pucky to dissect.

But finally his moment came. A single Springer rounded the corner and walked leisurely towards Pucky. Pucky leaped into hiding so as not to betray his presence prematurely. He sensed the man through the wall when he approached within 15 feet from him as he strolled along.

Pucky jumped back. He heard the tall husky Springer utter a startled cry and felt the fright suddenly springing up in his mind. Pucky raised his impulse-beamer, ready to shoot. The Springer was completely dumbfounded.

Pucky addressed him in Interkosmo: '*Exu*! you won't get hurt if you tell me quickly and precisely where the commander is.'

The mouse-beaver could see the whole spectrum of baffling and harrowing emotions flit by. 'Hurry up!' he urged. 'I'll shoot you before I'll let myself get caught because of you.'

The Springer got the point. But he was also aware of his duty to the security of his ship which forbade him to betray the whereabouts of his commander. However, as this very thought passed through his mind, it contained the information Pucky wanted and the Springer received the irritating advice: 'You can relax now, my boy! Etztak's command centre is located in the midsector of the main corridor. The door is clearly marked. Thank you! And what you were trying to think up just now, you can tell somebody else sometime.'

Then Pucky jumped back through the wall again. The information the man had given him was much more detailed than Pucky had repeated. He now knew exactly within a few feet where he could find Etztak and since the distance from his hide-out was rather short he could leap there directly in one jump. However, he required a moment of special concentration. It was possible that too many people were present in Etztak's command centre at the time he appeared, which would force him to jump back instantly. Furthermore he had to take into account that the Springer he had accosted just now would need only a limited time to assure himself that his meeting a furry animal in a spacesuit with extrasensory perception was not a dream. Doubtlessly he would report the incident without further delay.

Pucky knew very little about the customs of the Springers and could not guess how they would treat such sensational news. It was possible that they would simply ridicule and dismiss it or that Etztak would be notified at once. The mouse-beaver decided to consider the latter case as the more likely and hence haste was advisable.

He took a few seconds to concentrate and then took the jump.

'Let's go down!' Willagar said.

They set the ships cautiously down in the snow.

'Now what?' Horlgon asked.

Willagar laughed provocatively. 'One from each ship will have to get out and take a close look around.'

Horlgon was reluctant. 'But Etztak forbade us to leave the ship!'

'And how else does he suppose we can catch the escaped men?' Willagar challenged.

Horlgon didn't know how to answer his question so Willagar assumed that he concurred. 'How about the two of us, Horlgon?' he asked.

'All right,' Horlgon consented hesitantly and the tone of his voice indicated how much he disliked acting against the patriarch's orders.

'Let's go!' Willagar laughed.

'They landed after 12 minutes,' Tiff observed calmly. 'Can there be any doubt now that they've detected the ship?'

'No,' Eberhardt agreed.

Hifield said nothing. Tiff could hear him breathe heavily in the helmet radio.

'What are we going to do next?' Eberhardt wanted to know.

'Make sure that your deflector is working!' Tiff said. 'Let's first go and see what they're up to.'

They rose up from the snow and walked a few steps,

leaving footprints in the whiteness as the only eerie sign of their presence. They could not see each other due to deflector screens.

Tiff reminded the girls to remain quietly in the cave and he ordered Aubrey to stand by. The enemy was 1000 feet away. Tiff knew that Aubrey, despite his weight could cover this distance in a few moments and come to their aid should the need arise.

Then he instructed his two companions to actuate the antigrav. The generators began to work and a strong gravitational field lifted the cadets a few feet above the snow with the telltale footmarks. Then they drifted through the dusk towards the spot where, according to Aubrey, the patrol ships had landed.

'Activate your impact screens to be on the safe side!' Tiff said quietly. 'In case they should somehow notice us, they'll start shooting.'

The snow was very soft and they sank in up to their knees with each step. They were lucky, Horlgon thought, that the gravity was so low here or it would take them all night to slog through the snow. *Willagar seems to be too much in a hurry; he's very imprudent.*

After they had walked for 15 minutes and covered half the distance, Horlgon remarked: 'It's not wise to head straight for them like we're doing.'

Willagar stood still. 'What do you mean by that?'

Horlgon stretched out his gloved hands and turned the palms upward. 'They've got Arkonide spaceships and by the same token they could have field-generators and deflectors to make themselves invisible.'

Willagar laughed contemptuously. 'They came in a

tiny craft with no more than three seats and we've seen from their tracks that there are six persons. How much more equipment do you think they could've loaded in and dragged along?'

Horlgon kept his hands outstretched. 'I don't know. All I know is that it would be much smarter if we didn't head straight for them.'

Their conversation was audible via the helmet radio in both patrol ships. Psholgur sneered: 'Don't listen to him, Willagar! He's scared stiff, that's all.'

Willagar laughed again: 'Yeah! You hit it on the nose!'

Horlgon reacted to the reproach by defiantly marching ahead past Willagar. He still considered the action as perilous and reckless but he would rather die because of Willagar's bravado than be called a coward.

The orange-coloured sun provided just enough light to discern some of the features of the land as they drifted 20 feet above the ground. Tiff was able to make out two tall, powerful figures wading through the snow and sinking in deeply under their considerable weight as they were about 250 feet from the rim of the ravine and 150 feet from the entrance to the cave.

'Watch out!' Tiff whispered.

Eberhardt had already noticed them. Hifield turned up his horizontal drive and zoomed forward. Tiff didn't see him but he felt the gentle jolt when Hifield couldn't brake in time. 'Where?' Hifield panted.

Tiff didn't have to answer his question since Hifield saw the men at the same moment.

Later on it was impossible to find out what had motivated Hifield at this instant. Anyway, before Tiff or Eberhardt could prevent it, he pulled up his impulse-beamer and aimed it at the first of the two figures.

Horlgon was beyond help. The concentrated energy of the brilliant beam hit him before he had time to evade it. Willagar broke out in a loud scream and flung himself down. But his foe was a well-trained shot. Willagar was only half-submerged in the snow when the glistening beam found its second mark.

'Damn idiot!' Tiff yelled furiously. He threw a punch and struck somebody he thought was Hifield and kept pummelling. Hifield was shoved away and sailed topsy-turvy over the snow.

'Hurry!' Tiff shouted. 'Let's get the patrol ships before they make off!'

Hifield didn't hear a thing. It was Tiff and Eberhardt alone who raced swiftly to the spot where the patrol crafts had touched down.

Enaret heard Willagar's anguished cry and realized how right Etztak had been when he forbade leaving the ship. 'They got caught!' he called to Psholgur.

Psholgur had failed to grasp the situation. Enaret heard him calling monotonously: 'Willagar! Willagar! Horlgon! where are you?'

'They're dead!' Enaret shouted. 'Don't you understand that?'

He didn't wait for Psholgur's answer. Hastily he got ready to start and lifted his ship off the ground, expecting Psholgur to follow him. Enaret knew what he was up against. Two small patrol ships were no match against such an enemy. They needed more help.

He got up to 1000 feet and began to transmit the message: 'Patrol ships 31 and 32 made contact with enemy. Request assistance. Enemy is heavily armed. Position . . .'

He repeated the message five times and felt sure that his emergency call had been heard everywhere. Then he turned his attention to Psholgur again and saw his ship rise from the snow and rapidly gain height. For a few seconds it seemed that Psholgur had regained his wits and scrambled to escape from the danger zone. Instead the blue point on the observation screen moved to the side. Psholgur's ship ceased climbing and flew in a westerly direction following Willagar's and Horlgon's tracks.

'Come back, Psholgur!' Enaret shouted. 'Come back, you imbecile!'

But Psholgur didn't listen and gave no answer. With increasing speed his ship rushed towards west.

'Ship lifts off!' Aubrey reported with a monotone voice. 'Climbs rapidly.'

They must be scared, Tiff thought. *They don't know what they're getting into.*

A few seconds later Aubrey continued: 'Emergency call in Interkosmo!'

Tiff swore under his breath. In a few minutes the entire Springer pack would be at their heels through Hifield's fault.

Now the robot called out: 'Caution, sir! Second ship took off and is approaching you!'

Tiff acted at once. 'Move over to the right, Eberhardt!' he shouted.

Eberhardt complied immediately and Tiff heard him whizz by.

'Very good, sir,' Aubrey commented. 'The ship will pass you at a distance of 100 feet.'

'Let's get a little closer, Eberhardt!' Tiff said through his teeth.

They turned back a few more feet and then the ship arrived. Tiff could hear its whoosh and saw a dark shadow looming up a few feet before him. It was a vague target but . . .

Psholgur threw all caution to the winds. He didn't even know why he flew in this direction. He had been so convinced that the people they looked for were such poor, half-starved specimens of humanity that Willagar's and Horlgon's death had shocked him beyond the threshold of sanity. He yet saw for a fraction of a second the bluish white energy rays shooting towards his ship as they were reflected on his observation screen. And then it was all over.

Enaret watched the death of Psholgur. On his screen, which depicted nothing in the blackness of space except the faint orange blotch of the central sun, a glaring bright moving point suddenly appeared. He saw it plunge down into the snow and spring up like a fountain.

'Psholgur!'

The blinding point was extinguished and the silence of death reigned.

It took a few seconds before Tiff and Eberhardt fathomed that they had indeed shot down the hostile ship with their small thermobeamers. It had been their intention to disable the ship and to force it down but the full energy discharge of both weapons was sufficient to destroy the craft completely.

Tiff didn't waste his time examining the exploded ship after it crashed. Time was of the essence. 'Back to the cave, Eberhardt!' he bellowed. 'Turn off your deflector!'

Then Tiff increased the range of his transmitter and barked with undiminished fury: 'Hifield, get back to the cave and be quick about it!'

In a few minutes the Springers would be all over the place – hordes of them!

CHAPTER FOUR

PUCKY IN ACTION

Pucky's jump transported him into a small room of the navigation section. The room was only about 150 square feet. The walls were covered with maps of the stars and on a table, the only piece of furniture in the room, stood a mini-positronicomputer, probably for rough calculations of ship courses.

Pucky listened. He perceived a chaotic mass of thoughts emanating from the adjacent room through the wall. He started to sort out the impulses. He determined that four people were present in the other room. The attitude of three of them was easily recognized as caution mixed with respect, and antipathy which a man always feels towards a superior. Pucky classified them as obvious subordinates. Therefore, he concluded, the fourth man had to be the boss. It took barely a minute till the name of the superior officer was mentioned in one of the thoughts: Etztak!

The mouse-beaver sat down under the table and proceeded to separate and coördinate the stream of thought-impulses from the various minds and to form an understanding of the conversation conducted on the other side of the wall. The gist of it was:

'The reason,' one of the subaltern brains explained, 'was that Willagar and Horlgon left their vehicles against your orders, Sire.'

There were serveral other half-conscious and subconscious trains of thoughts such: 'I'd done the same thing in their place. Fortunately I was spared their fate!' But Pucky was mainly interested in the more significant clear thoughts that were the basis for the spoken words.

The answer came from the dominant mind: 'It's irrelevant now why the two ships bungled their job. I'm only interested in whether or not the fugitives will be caught.'

A second subordinate officer spoke up: 'We've expedited all ships to the critical area, Sire! They can't get away now!'

'Is that so?' Etztak asked derisively. 'Isn't that what you said before? Instead of getting your man you've succeeded in letting three of ours be killed and one patrol ship be destroyed.'

There was a pause during which Pucky only perceived some extremely embarrassed thoughts. Then Etztak continued: 'I don't mind telling you that those fugitives are very important to me but not so important as to let them lead me by the nose indefinitely. If this action doesn't bring results soon I'll turn this whole world into a blazing sun!'

Pucky noted grave bewilderment. Etztak apparently dismissed his officers. There was some movement and the old man remained alone in the room. The mouse-beaver received only his thoughts after the three others had moved far enough down the hallway.

And the contents of Etztak's deliberations raised horrendous fears in the little mouse-beaver. Etztak had not spoken empty threats when he warned about a demolition of the planet. He really mulled over this thought and Pucky was able to learn his motives.

We can't afford, Etztak pondered, *to spend too much time searching this planet. It'll draw the others' attention and if they become aroused they'll smell a profit and try to snatch it out of our hands. Whatever we can pry loose from Tifflor we should certainly be able to dig up on his home world. The* HORL VII *had enough Arkon bombs on board to change this planet into radiating energy. Then nobody will have an opportunity to lay his hands on Tifflor and get information out of him.*

Pucky was alerted by the ominous signs of danger from two sides. First of all, there was apparently a concerted search effort under way for Tifflor and his people and it seemed to have met already with partial success. And secondly, Etztak was ready to exterminate Snowman if Tiff were to prevail over his hunters against all expectations and to thwart their initial advantages.

The mouse-beaver faced a dilemma and it was difficult for him to decide which action to take first. He could pay a visit to the HORL VII – which according to Etztak's information was standing by 250 miles out in space – and deactivate its load of bombs. But meanwhile Tiff and his people were likely to be apprehended and to liberate them again once they were brought back to the ship would be an incomparably more difficult task than to rush to their aid now.

Thus he decided to abandon the ETZ XXI and to return to the cave. If he managed to join the fight quickly enough and to influence its outcome favourably, there would still be time to spoil Etztak's plan and to eliminate the danger threatening from the Arkon bombs of the HORL VII.

Crouching under the table he focused on the mountain cave where the cadets and the girls were hiding.

And jumped off.

Exhausted and sleepy, Reginald Bell returned on board the *Stardust* in the Z-13. Nothing he would have liked better than to hit the hay for the next 20 hours. Instead he took the tape he had dictated on the flight out of the recorder and put it in his pocket. After climbing out of his machine he went to the elevator and up to the command centre.

Perry Rhodan was already waiting for him. Bell gave a short report and referred to the tape for more explicit details.

After Bell's audacious reconnaissance flight it was determined that the two fleets of Springer ships which had come to the Beta–Albireo sector were in fact two completely separate and independent outfits. The vessels with which Bell had tangled were merchant ships identifiable by their shape. They had taken up position on or near the surface of the planet serving as refuge for Tifflor. This group consisted of 78 ships and nobody knew who owned them.

The second group numbering 90 ships had been

evaded by Bell in his turning manoeuvre. Their shape marked them as warships. They were not quite as long as the merchant ships and a little plumper. They belonged to the same armada as the 30 warships which had 100 hours ago caught hell from the *Stardust*, the *Terra* and the *Solar System.*

There was no visible connection between the two fleets. Unless they exchanged information among each other, they operated completely on their own.

Bell had no doubt – and he was quite emphatic about it – that the 90 warships after the tumult caused by the Z-13 would soon endeavour to locate the opponent. He believed that they would fan out and comb the system in small groups.

'If we get into a brush with them, we better look out,' Bell prophesied. 'I don't believe we've much of a chance against them in open battle.'

'They're coming!' Aubrey reported. 'Twenty-four machines!'

They had returned to their shelter and closed the partitions behind them. Hifield had come back before them. His triumphant euphoria had cooled and given way to a gloomy depression.

'In the first hour,' Tiff pointed out quietly, 'they won't bother us. They'll stay in their ships and look for our hide-out which they're sure to find since the outer cover can be easily recognized if they come near enough. Even then, I'd think, we won't have to fear very much. The deflector screens make us invisible and the impact screens protect us against shots from many diversified weapons. Moreover, the Springers are more anxious to capture us than to kill us.

Tiff paused and looked around. 'But I'm afraid,' he continued, 'they'll run out of patience and bombard us with weapons which cannot be repulsed by our impact screens. Therefore we'll have to get out of here and the sooner the better. The longer we lead the Springers astray the easier it'll be for us to reach safety.'

Hifield and Eberhardt nodded. The girls stared with wide eyes and Aubrey stood rigidly, his head slightly leaning back as if he studied the ceiling.

'But how,' Eberhardt asked after a while, 'can we steal away without being seen? If Aubrey is right they're already on top of us.'

Tiff smiled a little superciliously, intimating that he had a plan all figured out already. 'We're going to exit through there and disappear,' he said, pointing over his shoulder to the rear wall of the cave.

Eberhardt looked around. 'That way?' His eyes wandered back again and he stared at Tiff's smiling face.

'How do you want to accomplish that?' Hump murmured in the background.

Instead of replying Tiff turned to RB-013. 'Aubrey, where are they?'

'Exactly over the spot where you've shot down the machine, sir! They're stopped and are staggered in clusters of four, one above the other. The lowest group is 80 feet and the highest 600 feet above the ground.'

'All right, Aubrey! Go ahead!' Tiff ordered.

Aubrey stirred from his rigid stance. With an agility nobody would have suspected in the tons of metal he wheeled around, he took a few crunching steps towards the rear wall of the cave and raised his left weapon arm.

RB-013 had four arms – two on each side. The upper pair of arms served the same purpose as human arms. The lower arms were nothing but a pair of movable cannons, a disintegrator on one side and a thermo-beamer on the other.

Faintly glowing greenish energy rays shot from the muzzle of the arm. The rock of the wall melted like snow in the sun. Actually it did not really melt. The effect of the disintegrator stemmed from the fact that the crystallizing forces of solid matter were annulled in the field of the disintegrator. Atoms and molecules became separated and the exposed radiated matter turned into gas – or plasma when applying high-yield disintegrators.

'Close your helmets!' Tiff ordered as the others watched with fascination the robot doing his work. Clouds of stone dust drifted through the cave, entered their noses and created a feeling of suffocation in their lungs. They locked their helmets when they noticed that breathing became dangerous and kept staring at the hole penetrating deeper and deeper into the rock under the powerful beam of the disintegrator.

'Okay.' Tiff smiled. 'You've seen enough now. There are more disintegrators in Pucky's supplies. Take one each and help Aubrey with the work. We have to push through in a hurry.'

Under Tiff's direction the beams of the five disintegrators were distributed over an area six feet high and three wide. The weapons operating at peak efficiency ate into the rock at the rate of eight inches per second. The passage through which Tiff hoped to slip away from the Springers grew rapidly.

Tiff didn't take part in the job of gouging out the passage. He rummaged through the store of equipment brought by Pucky and picked out a number of devices resembling hand grenades. They were indeed hand grenades but instead of a charge of powder they contained a highly efficient gravity generator. The generator had only an operating span of one-thousandth of a second. But in the course of this short interval it created a gravitational field of considerable magnitude. The strong field and its explosive nature made it an extremely effective weapon for close combat.

It was Tiff's assumption that the Springers were bound to detect the cave sooner or later and to invade it. Furthermore they were certain to find the passage the disintegrators carved into the stone wall and they had only to follow them through the passage to be sure to stay on their heels and to overtake them again. Therefore, the cave and the entrance of the passage had to be erased. This was, of course, a very easy matter. The small grenades were equipped with simple but adequate time fuses serving Tiff's purpose perfectly. He only had to place the hand grenade in a crevice and run into the passage.

If only Pucky were back already! When he returned from his reconnaissance trip he would select the cave as point of entry for his teleportation and Tiff didn't want to run the risk of letting him plunge into the middle of the exploding cave or fall into the hands of the advancing Springers. The time Pucky had set for his return had not yet expired. There was still half an hour left and Tiff was determined to wait for him, come what might.

He didn't have to worry about Aubrey and his companions. With Aubrey leading the way they would have blasted out 1200 feet in another half an hour. That was far enough to be a safe distance.

Tiff had been told by Pucky about the cell transmitter for telepaths implanted in his body without his knowledge. He now knew that Pucky could trace him anywhere within a radius of two light-years. If he followed the others into the shaft and thereby indicated to Pucky that he was no longer in the cave, there was a possibility that the mouse-beaver would perhaps change the goal of his teleportation.

Perhaps! Perhaps only sheer speculation! He had to wait and see how the situation developed . . .

Enaret reported for the fifth time what he had observed. 'Yes, that's where Psholgur's ship plummeted down. You can tell where the sheet of ice is. No, not over there. That's where Willagar was shot. Yes. No, there's no trace of Horlgon.'

Etztak had put a man by the name of Wernal in charge of the 24 ships. Enaret considered him not too bright but he was careful to keep his opinion to himself.

As long as Enaret didn't have to give explanations he kept his eyes on the sensor screen. In his judgment it was useless to waste time hovering over the scene of the disaster and to search for the tracks of Psholgur, Horlgon and Willagar. What they wanted to find was the strangers, not the dead!

But Wernal was in command and he thought that his strategy was the only sound one. Until Enaret believed he had suddenly found what he was looking for.

The sensor screen depicted a steeply rising wall of the mountain. Enaret clearly discerned a funnel-shaped outline of what seemed to be the entrance to a cave. And a few feet behind the rim of the funnel the sensor beam reflected some compact matter. A wall!

Enaret was thinking fast. What kind of a cave could this be that formed a deep funnel in the mountain side and ended only a few feet behind the funnel's rim? He concluded that the wall behind the funnel was an artificial structure.

He contacted Wernal and advised him of his findings. Wernal was not exactly overjoyed that one of his subordinates had apparently made an important discovery without him but he nonetheless paid careful attention and became convinced that Enaret was probably right. There must indeed be a cave in the mountain before them and the cave was shielded from the outside world by an artificial wall. Wernal pointed in the direction and ordered: 'We're moving in and we'll land in a semi-circle around the cave at a distance of 200 feet!'

Tiff heard Aubrey's announcement via helmet radio: 'They're coming, sir! They've landed in front of the cave!'

Tiff answered tersely: 'I get it! Just keep going with your work!'

So they've found us, he thought grimly. Another 15 minutes had elapsed. Unless he was able to hold out long enough, Pucky would . . .

Tiff carefully checked the controls of his transport suit. At the end he left his deflector and impact screen in activated state. He cradled in his left arm the heavy thermobeamer taken from Pucky's armaments and pushed the cover plate of the inner partition out with his right hand. He could feel the floor quake as the heavy stone hit it. In the light of the last emergency lamp he could see the second partition wall which was only 10 feet away. At this distance an automatic thermobeamer could rain dreadful destruction.

Let them come!

All of a sudden Wernal was in a great hurry. 'Send out one man from each ship!' he ordered. 'Enaret, take the men to the cave. Exercise caution when breaking in and remember, we want to get the strangers alive if possible!'

Enaret left his ship where it was and climbed out. He gathered all the men who had disembarked around him. While Wernal was running out of patience Enaret deemed it important to point out to the men that they faced a wily enemy. 'Unquestionably they've deflector screens, perhaps even antigrav generators and certainly very sophisticated weapons. Furthermore they're in such a desperate position that they can't afford to pull their punches.

They'll shoot when they see the enemy. Keep that in mind and don't try to be heroic!'

Then they advanced towards the entrance of the cave.

Tiff noticed it when they started to work at the outside of the cave. As soon as they had found the cover plate the ground ceased shaking. Perhaps it would take them longer than the remaining time set for Pucky's return!

Where was Pucky?

The great number of walls disturbed Enaret since he had not yet figured out what purpose they served.

Wernal kept urging from a safe place: 'Make it snappy! Go on!'

Enaret looked at his men. In the light of his little lamp he could see them grin behind the clear faceplates of their helmets. 'Keep going!' he growled.

The aliens had built the thin partitions from one wall to within three feet of the opposite one and covered the remaining space with molten stone plates. Enaret was amazed how well these pieces fitted into the grooves of the partitions and side walls. The inserts were so constructed that they could be put in place or be removed from either side. In order to save time, Enaret instructed his men to push the covers inward with a quick hard blow and to jump back to the side in case the enemy was lying in wait behind it.

The method worked very well and they went from wall to wall without running into resistance when one of the men finally called out in surprise: 'The cover plate in the next wall is missing and a light is burning behind it!'

Even then the hidden foe didn't reveal himself and Enaret began to suspect a trap. Or did the cave have another exit?

He squeezed past his men and leaned forward to look around the partition. He saw the next wall and the opening which had held the inserted plate before. Now the cover lay on the floor. Through the hole Enaret recognized a spacious, faintly lit room. A single lamp provided some sort of an emergency light. The shaft which had been cut into the rock by the disintegrators was concealed from his view by the partition.

'Let's go on!' Enaret commanded.

Tiff heard the muffled rumbling when the piece in the next to last partition was knocked out. He drew his weapon closer so that the muzzle of the barrel was pulled back inside the deflector field and became totally invisible. He saw Enaret when he showed his head at the edge of the partition to survey the cave.

There were still four minutes to go before the half hour was up. The hand grenades were set to detonate 10 minutes after the expiration of the deadline. If Pucky failed to return on time, the terror Tiff planned to strike into the Springers would have to last at least 10 minutes.

And now they infiltrated. Cautiously they sneaked around the partition and quickly leaped away to the side.

Tiff raised the barrel of his heavy weapon but he had no desire to kill them. He squeezed the trigger and fired a low energy shot against the rock. The effect was spectacular. From one moment to the next the ceiling began to glow, to melt and to evaporate. White hot rocks came tumbling down, sizzled and hissed when they hit the cold ground, raining a shower of sparks in all directions. Vapours filled the chamber and blurred all outlines. Tiff saw darting shadows fleeing in wild haste around the next partition to escape the rampant pyrotechnics.

Laughingly he blasted another shot at the partition. Instantly it turned into a glowing liquid mass, buckled and collapsed, rendering the third wall behind it visible through green vapours released from the stone. The Springers were in hasty retreat. Tiff saw the last one of them scrambling through the opening and he also shot up the third partition close behind them.

At this moment he heard in his speaker a whimsical voice: 'Good work, my boy!'

He whirled around. In the middle of the cave under the last lamp sat Pucky. Tiff sighed with relief and switched off his deflector field so that Lucky could see him. He started to give some hasty explanations but Pucky waved his hand nonchalantly in a human gesture. 'I know all about it. I can read your thoughts clearly. Leave this place at once! I'll take over your position and hold it for a while.'

Tiff understood his reasons. It was crucial for Tiff to use his legs to put the greatest possible distance between himself and the cave before the time of the explosion. By contrast, Pucky would be able to leap across the distance in one jump and the cell transmitter Tiff carried in his body would guide him precisely.

'The grenade is set to go off in 10 minutes,' Tiff panted.

Pucky nodded and hopped to the inner partition taking Tiff's place. 'Now get lost!' he lisped.

Tiff ran. The passage burned out by the disintegrators was spacious enough to allow him to skip out in a sprint.

The real danger which Tiff had kept in mind all along was not from the explosion itself but from its secondary effects. The gravitation field produced by the hand grenades was very powerful but of limited range. For a person in the shaft more than 150 feet away from the explosion, the suction wave moving from the depth of the shaft towards the origin of the explosion constituted the greatest peril.

Tiff stormed along the shaft. Aubrey reported to him that they had encountered less resistant rock and that they were now 2000 feet away from the cave.

Tiff tried briefly to use the transport suit for his getaway but it turned out that the passage was too narrow for the suit to serve as an efficient means of locomotion. Three minutes after he had left Pucky he reached the cadets and the girls. He had already brought them abreast during his run about the events taking place in the cave. Tiff quickly took over the disintegrator from Mildred. She was glad to hand him the weapon and be relieved of the work.

'I'm happy you made it,' she said softly. Tiff lifted his head in surprise and looked at her. He saw her big shining eyes behind her helmet's visor and replied a little awkwardly: 'Yes, so am I.'

He squeezed the disintegrator firmly under his arm and started to blast away at the rock.

One minute before the explosion Tiff stopped all work and made everybody lie down flat on the ground. Five seconds before zero Pucky materialized in midair and a few moments later the prostrate figures seemed gripped by a mighty fist as a thunderous tremor shook the mountain.

Then it was all over and they rose again.

'Everything appears to be all right,' Pucky said. 'The Springers never came back and now they can't find us any more.'

He related briefly what he had experienced on board the ETZ XXI and concluded his report: 'None of them realizes how well a good telepath can judge the character of an intelligent being. I am certain that the old man won't hesitate for a moment to blow this world to smithereens. If Etztak finds out that his latest foray has failed again he'll be burned up and furious enough to order the final demolition of this planet. We can't lose another minute. We must infiltrate the HORL VII and ETZ XXI without delay.'

Tiff had listened attentively. 'Why do we have to get on board the ETZ XII, sir?' he asked.

Pucky peeped a cry and explained: 'To take Etztak as prisoner in case we don't succeed in preventing the HORL VII from launching its bombs. I suggest that we surface as fast as possible and get on our way. We know the layout of the Springer ships and you'll be able to orient yourselves on board with my specifications.'

They surfaced one mile north of the cave at the northern slope of the mountain. Pucky had first made sure that the coast was clear by teleporting himself for short jumps out of the shaft. He also had made a short foray to the cave and returned with the news that the Springers were now busy poking through the remnants of the stone walls. He estimated that it would take at least another hour before Etztak would be informed of the failure of their mission. Pucky perceived from the minds of the Springers that they were reluctant to believe the version of the suicide of the doomed aliens. However, somebody by the name of Wernal had given the order to search for the remains of the strangers.

'That ought to keep them busy for quite a while,' Pucky piped. 'In the meantime we'll make headway.'

The two girls were left behind with Aubrey. The robot received orders to widen the exit of the shaft so that it could be used as a temporary base. Pucky made it clear to Aubrey that it was preferable to surrender with the two girls than risk that the Springers would drop a bomb on the exit.

Then Pucky and the three cadets started out on their trek. Pucky, clad in a simple spacesuit, teleported himself ahead of the others for some distance and waited for the cadets to catch up with him by flying rapidly and low above the snow. In this manner it took them a few hours to approach within 12 miles of the place where the two Springer ships had landed. The night would still last a few more hours so that they could at least begin their action under the protection of darkness.

While the three cadets remained at a safe distance Pucky teleported himself with a well-aimed jump on board the ETZ XXI. Unabashed and without a slip-up he locked the hangar officer of the gigantic ship in his own office and forced him to release one of the patrol ships and to advise the HORL VII of the arrival of a ship so that thc HORL VII would open its hangar in response to the code signal without making further inquiries. Then he took the patrol ship and returned to the waiting cadets.

'One of you,' Pucky said, 'Is coming with me. The other two will fly to the HORL VII. The Arkon bombs are kept in storeroom No. 78 on the fifth deck from the hangar. You'll have no trouble finding your way. It is necessary that you get there in 10 minutes. The hangar officer of the ETZ XXI is unconscious and I've dragged him to some place where they won't find him so soon. But after a while he's going to wake up and tell old Etztak what has happened. You'll have to be on board the HORL by that time. They'll sound the alarm on it as soon as the hangar officer is heard from. It won't be an easy job for you but you know what's at stake. Now please decide who'll accompany me and who's flying to the HORL.'

It was truly amazing how easy it was to forget that Pucky was not a human being when he spoke so seriously and to the point as at this moment.

Tiff looked at the two cadets. 'I'd like to take Cadet Hifield to the HORL,' Tiff proposed.

Eberhardt and Hifield both looked surprised and so was Pucky as he gazed from one to the other.

No wonder, Tiff thought with amusement, *he can read what is going on in our minds.*

'Cadet Hifield?' Pucky snorted.

'Yes, sir!'

'Are you ready?'

'Yes, sir!'

'Okay, let's get started. We've got to hurry up!'

As Tiff passed Eberhardt he slapped him on the shoulder. 'Take care!' he said softly. He was convinced that Eberhardt understood why he took Hifield instead of him. Hifield should get one more chance.

Etztak's fury was boundless. He stood in the middle of the oval command centre and raved violently. His majestic voice filled the room.

An hour ago a man called Frerfak had told him a story about a furry animal he had encountered in a side corridor who had demanded information as to the exact location of the command centre. The animal, so Frerfak claimed, was a telepath as well as a teleporter.

Etztak was outraged and threw the man out telling him in no uncertain terms that liars would be severely dealt with on board his ship.

In Etztak's opinion there were beings present in the Galaxy who distinguished themselves by one or another unusual ability. They were either telepaths or telekineticists or teleporters. But a creature who was a telepath as *well* as a teleporter had never been seen by Etztak. Therefore he didn't believe in the existence of such an extraordinary freak of nature and he assumed that Frerfak had a vivid imagination.

However, half an hour after Frerfak's tale Holloran appeared in the command centre, bothered by his conscience. He described how a creature who perfectly resembled Frerfak's 'freak' had forced him to be taken aboard the ETZ XXI in his patrol ship. Nor did Holloran's description leave any doubt that the stranger was a teleporter and a telepath too. Etztak's preconceived ideas were already beginning to waver.

Twenty minutes after Holloran's narration, Wernal reported via telecom about the debacle of his search expedition and minutes later the officer in charge of the hangar operations related his weird story of being pressured into releasing one of the patrol ships and having to inform the HORL VII of the imminent arrival of the craft yielded by him.

As a consequence Etztak's mental balance was badly shattered. He began to rant, shouting orders to his men, countermanding them before they could be passed on. It took him several minutes to calm down sufficiently. Finally he was able to make some sensible decisions and to transmit them clearly:

'Alert the HORL VII! Warn them of probable intruders. Direct the HORL VII to land at once and to safeguard its bombs which we want to use to destroy this world!'

The draconic order was relayed to the HORL VII and confirmed. They verified that a patrol ship had been admitted a few minutes earlier after they had been advised of the flight, that it had given the proper code signal and that it had been berthed promptly.

The captain of the HORL VII, Horlagan, was severely shaken up by the warning. He reported back that he had immediately initiated a thorough search and was ready to land.

CHAPTER FIVE

LET SLEEPING MYSTERIES LIE?

All went smoothly. The patrol ship passed through both hatches of the airlock, entered the tunnel to the hangar and was steered automatically to a vacant pad. Following Pucky's instructions Tiff announced in Interkosmo over the telecom to the hangar supervisor that he had secured his craft in place and asked permission for himself and his companion to ride up in the ship.

The hangar supervisor approved routinely. The fact that Tiff used the space-wide language was not noteworthy. Only few Springers still used their own national language. As a general rule for convenience sake they had adopted Interkosmo, even among each other.

Aided by Pucky's graphic description Tiff and Hifield had little trouble making their way through the vessel. It was also helpful that Tiff had several times visited a Springer ship – the ORLA XI – and that the Springers favoured a systematic and functional arrangement for their ships.

Without being detected the two cadets went up as far as the third deck by using the big freight elevator shaft to which no person was admitted under the strict rules. At the height of the third deck they were in danger of colliding with a load floating down from above. The huge load filled the shaft so completely that there was no gap left big enough for Tiff and Hifield to squeeze through. They had no choice other than to escape from the shaft through a door to a gangway on the third deck. The load slid farther down and just at the moment when they thought that the danger had passed another threat appeared in the person of a Springer rounding the corner of the gangway and walking rapidly towards the shaft.

Hifield jumped him from the side and knocked him down with the butt of his weapon. Tiff's help was not needed.

'Where can we dump him?' Hifield panted.

Tiff tried to guess how long the Springer would remain unconscious. Twenty minutes? Perhaps half an hour?

He walked to the next hatch door, raised his thermo-beamer and let the door slide open. The room behind it was small and empty. 'Let's hide him in here,' Tiff whispered.

Hifield dragged the unconscious man over. Together they stowed him away in the little chamber and closed the hatch again.

'Move on!'

Without further mishap they reached the fifth deck. According to Pucky's survey the store room was located a little more than 150 feet from the exit to the antigrav shaft. They had to pass through a narrow, twisting corridor. There were no obstacles around the exit of the shaft but after listening for a few seconds they could hear the babble of voices farther in the background.

'Let's go!'

They held their weapons ready to shoot and scurried down the corridor. Tiff figured that the corridor was lined with storage rooms and that they would have a chance to run inside in case they encountered another Springer.

After they had passed around three corners they found a bunch of Springers coming their way.

'To the left!' Tiff grunted.

The hatch slowly opened up. Hump squeezed through first and groaned as he nearly crushed his chest. Tiff followed him, taking a last look along the corridor. There was no sign that the Springers had discovered them.

Tiff turned around. He stood behind Hifield's broad back and murmured: 'Saved in the nick of time . . .'

Hifield acted very oddly – as if he were scared! Tiff leaned to the side and peeked around him.

Ten feet before Hifield stood a Springer with the funnel-shaped barrel of his weapon trained on Hifield's belly. It was only one man but he had the advantage that he had already raised his gun, ready to shoot.

Tiff looked around. The room was full of shelves and automatic sorting machines were mounted on the upper edges of the racks. The machines were made to move up and down on vertical rails. The shelves were stocked with parts, measuring instruments and switch units. Tiff was standing next to a rack and he only needed to reach out his hand to touch it.

'*Vantu,*' Hifield asked hoarsely in Interkosmo. 'What do you want?'

The Springer began to laugh. 'I want to know who you are and what you're doing here.'

Hifield scraped the floor with one foot. Tiff got the signal. Hifield planned to distract the Springer and it was up to Tiff to make use of the feint. Hundreds of thoughts flashed through Tiff's mind but none of them was practical.

'None?'

Tiff leaned to the left towards the rack. From the corner of his eye he could see that he was able to reach the sorting machine which had been left at a lower shelf after its last use. Cautiously he began to stretch his hand towards the machine while endeavouring to remain out of sight behind Hifield's back.

It'll be too bad for you, Springer, Tiff thought grimly, *if you don't know how dangerous it is to line up two enemies behind each other!*

'I can answer that question easily,' Hifield replied. Tiff who knew him so well could tell from his voice how keyed up he was.

Steady, Hifield! Tiff kept thinking. *Here's the switch.* The switch clicked softly as he flipped it. The machine started to hum and glided swiftly up the rail. The Springer was startled and glanced sideways. Tiff stepped to the right, pulled up the barrel of his weapon and fired.

The Springer was killed on the spot. Tiff and

Hifield remained still for a few moments, unable to move.

'Let's get out of here!' Tiff urged, the first to regain his composure. As cautiously as they could in their excitement they opened the hatch. The corridor was empty. They hurried on past the next corner and another one . . .

There it was! Number 78 written in Interkosmo letters on the strong metal doors of a large hatch. The hatch opened just like the others. There was nothing to indicate the special importance of its contents. Tiff had expected to find guards stationed in front of the hatch doors or behind them but none were present. The mentality of the Springers was obviously unencumbered by fear of abuse of the most terrifying weapon they had ever built.

The room was smaller than Tiff had imagined. The bombs, which were five foot long metallic cylinders with rounded ends, were each stored in separate fixtures of tough plastic metal.

Tiff locked the doors of the hatch behind him and watched how Hifield cautiously removed one of the bombs from the fixture and weighed it in his arms. He panted a little but when he turned around he grinned: 'I'd guess they weigh about 175 pounds. Not too heavy to be carried!'

'Now it's about time for Pucky to do his job,' Tiff replied.

With his abundance of parapsychological talents Pucky helped Cadet Eberhardt to board the ETZ XXI in one elegant jump. Pucky moved him in the same manner which he had used a day earlier to transport the bales from the Z-13 to Snowman – by teleportation.

Eberhardt landed in the hangar tunnel and crawled into one of the empty pads. Pucky appeared right behind him, made a mental note of the location of his hideout and vanished again.

Pucky held Eberhardt in reserve and he only intended to call him into the fight if the circumstances required his assistance. Now that he knew his whereabouts he was always in a position to contact him.

On the other hand, if anything happened to Pucky, Eberhardt could probably easily manage to seize one of the patrol ships and leave the ETZ XXI unmolested. For the time being, however, Pucky had no doubt that he could accomplish his purpose with no trouble at all.

When Pucky materialized again he stood in a little room adjacent to the command centre and separated from it only by a thin wall. Out of the flood of obtuse thoughts – mostly fearful and anguished – emanating from the command centre he quickly isolated Etztak's impulses.

Etztak felt in the middle of his outburst that a mysterious force reached for him. Completely vexed he fell silent, tried for a few moments to analyse his impressions and felt fear well up in him. He wanted to scream and when he did he was no longer in the command centre yet he had noticed no movement. It was as if one curtain had been pulled away from his face and another dropped behind him.

Etztak was familiar with the room, which was next to the command centre. What he didn't know was how he got there.

None of the men present in the command centre worried about his sudden disappearance. In the first place they enjoyed the silence and secondly, Etztak had been standing near a hatch while the officers were bent over their tables ostentatiously engrossed in their work. He could very well have slipped out of the room without being noticed which was what Pucky had hoped although he was not quite sure that this would work out.

Etztak's scream became suddenly stuck in his throat when he saw the furry little animal sitting on a table in front of him. He sat on his hindlegs with his body erect, holding in his right paw a little impulse beamer. Nobody had ever seen Etztak as flabbergasted as he was at this moment.

'Get hold of yourself!' Etztak understood. 'I've got to have a little talk with you.'

The bluntness of this approach brought Etztak to his senses. He wanted to flare up but the stranger didn't give him the opportunity. And he also explained why. 'It's imperative that we act fast,' Etztak was given to understand. 'Two of my men are on board the HORL VIII right now and as a result of the alarm you've called' – a fact which Pucky read in Etztak's mind – 'they're unable to leave the ship without hindrance.'

Etztak twisted his face into a jeering grin.

'You'll see to it that they're able to leave the ship without getting hurt!' Pucky continued.

Etztak started to laugh. 'And what if I don't?' he inquired.

'Then I'll blow up the whole shebang, the ORLA, the ETZ, the HORL and the whole planet!'

Etztak became serious. 'And how do you propose to do that?'

Pucky whistled shrilly: 'Exactly the same way *you* wanted to do it. With Arkon bombs!'

Etztak shuddered. 'You'd be killing yourself and your people too!'

'That's right!' Pucky answered simply. 'It's that important to us.'

Pucky sensed how Etztak desperately tried to find a way out. He could also feel the desire of the old man to procrastinate and to gain time by prolonging the conversation.

'Quit stalling!' Pucky urged, raising the impulse beamer and aiming above Etztak's left shoulder. He fired a short burst of low energy against the wall. Etztak winced and raised his hands.

'No!' he panted. 'I'll do what you want!'

Pucky determined immediately that he meant what he said.

'I'll give the HORL instructions to break off the search and to cancel the alarm,' Etztak suggested.

Pucky refused to agree. Not because he was afraid that the old man would play a trick on him but because he realized the uncertainty and confusion which would be caused by two contradictory orders following each other in short succession.

'No! You order a full battle alert for the HORL. Every man on his post and all men off duty to stand by in reserve. And do it right here! Do you follow me?'

Etztak hesitated. Pucky raised his weapon again and thereby broke the resistance of the old man. Etztak went to the intercom and took the microphone. Pucky placed himself outside the range of the receiver and made it clear to the Springer that he was prepared to shoot if he said as much as one wrong word.

For a few minutes the floor reverberated from the clatter of numerous feet running around in the corridors. But suddenly everything fell silent and then came Pucky's short message: 'All clear!'

Tiff let the hatch slide open. Hifield staggered through the opening and Tiff closed the door carefully. Then he rushed over to Hump to help him carry the bomb.

The HORL was in full battle alert which meant that nobody was around in the vicinity of the storerooms.

Without harassment they reached the shaft of the freight elevator in which they had ascended half an hour earlier. Breathing heavily Hifield tumbled into the antigrav field with his bomb and was slowly carried down the shaft with Tiff in tow.

'Stop at the second deck!' Tiff told Hifield. As they came abreast of the deck Hifield pushed himself away from the wall to leave through the exit.

'We'll have to go at least 150 feet from here,' Tiff said.

The corridor was empty. Tiff deciphered the markings on a hatch and determined that they were in an area of a hospital. If Pucky's plan worked all right, the Springers would remain behind the hatches without venturing into the corridors during the alarm unless they were called out.

Hifield reeled along the hallway. The inscriptions on the hatches were of a great variety. One of them read: Food & Drug Laboratory.

'In there!' Tiff ordered.

The vessel was a merchant ship. But even these merchant ships were armed to a certain degree and Tiff knew that everybody had been assigned a post in case of alarm. It was unlikely that they would find a Springer at this time in a lab for analysing unknown foods and drugs.

And so it was. The lab was rather spacious and equipped with all sorts of devices. Tiff directed Hifield to place the bomb on its end near a dehydration machine consisting of four cylindrical containers. There the bomb looked every inconspicuous.

'Set the timer for 20 minutes!' Tiff said, helping Hifield with the fuse. The trigger mechanism of the bomb was not very complicated.

'Ready!' Hifield reported. 'Let's get out of here!'

They returned to the antigrav elevator and went down to the hangar deck. Hastily, but almost noiselessly, they stormed through the gangway to the inner airlock hatch where the hangar officer had his control room.

During the state of alarm it would have been an impermissible infraction of regulations for the hangar supervisor to release a patrol ship via the usual procedure. The officer was alone with his assistant. Tiff and Hifield entered the little room without being challenged. The hangar master noticed only after they got in that they were strangers and the assistant never knew what happened. Tiff put the assistant out of action with a well-aimed blow against the collar of his protective suit. Hifield darted behind the desk and struck down the hangar officer before he was able to defend himself or call for help.

Tiff was already busy with the next task. He leaped with two quick steps to the huge control panel and pulled two well-marked red levers.

'The inner hatch is open!' he called to Hifield. 'Now to the patrol ships!'

Hifield dashed out. A few moments later the lentil-shaped body of a patrol ship glided through the hangar tunnel and moved through the open hatch into the air-lock, where it stopped. The canopy opened and Tiff clambered aboard by pulling himself up over its rim.

'Let's get on with it!'

Hifield started up again and moved across the vast airlock just at the moment when the inner hatch closed and the outer one slid open in accordance with the signal Tiff had actuated on the control panel. The little ship scooted outside and left the HORL behind.

Tiff cried out in surprise when he noticed that the big ship was only six miles above the surface of Snowman. The landing manoeuvre would be over in a few minutes.

Tiff turned on his helmet radio to long distance. 'It's all right, sir!' he reported as previously arranged.

He looked at his watch and added: 'Twelve minutes to zero!'

Pucky whistled with satisfaction when he got the message. 'Very good!' He let Etztak know that his men were free. 'And now I want to tell you something else.'

Etztak perked up.

'My men have stashed away somewhere on board the HORL an Arkon bomb and set the time fuse for 20 minutes, nine of which have already elapsed. The ETZ and the ORLA have now exactly 11 minutes to get out of here and the crew of the HORL must leave ship in their patrol crafts before the time is up to save their lives!'

Pucky said no more. He vanished instantaneously but he was sure that Etztak would heed his warning. He jumped without further delay to Klaus Eberhardt's hiding place. Eberhardt leaped down from the pad. Pucky looked around and found a patrol ship ready to go in one of the other pads. He hopped in and moved the ship into the tunnel. He took Eberhardt aboard after the cadet had advised the hangar officer and complied with the usual routine of taking out a patrol ship, requesting the opening of the air-lock.

For a few seconds Pucky feared that Etztak would have overcome his shock too soon and prevented the hangar master from letting them go. But his fear proved to be unfounded. The hatches opened and closed smoothly and the little ship shot out into the icy grey morning. Tiff and Hifield showed up with their ship at almost the same time.

'Back to Aubrey's cave!' Pucky commanded.

The flight took a few minutes. Pucky used the time to brief the cadets about the various contingencies in case his plan did not work out as expected. Tiff and Hifield listened to the lisping voice coming out of the loudspeaker during the short flight:

'The worst possibility would be that the crew of the HORL finds the bomb. However, this is not very likely when you consider that a ship like the HORL has about 5000 separate rooms and they've only 11 minutes for the search.

'The second possibility is that Etztak believes my threat was a bluff and does nothing about it. In this case the three ships will be completely destroyed in a few minutes. They're too close together for one of the ships to survive the catastrophe.

'And the third possibility would occur if Etztak takes my warning seriously but steers the two imperilled vessels away from the danger zone and has the HORL evacuated. Then he could perhaps take up his hunt for us again and we would have to defend ourselves.

'At any rate, we won't be able to stay very long in Aubrey's cave. We'll have to leave it before Etztak recovers from his distress because he's bound to resume the chase again sooner or later. Now we've got two patrol ships. Each is big enough to hold three people if necessary, which is sufficient if I travel by teleportation. We can fly back later to pick up the equipment we've saved.

'That'll be all we've to worry about for the time

being. Let's hope they don't stumble onto the bomb!'

Shortly before the landing the sensor instruments registered wild movements in the north. Two large vessels lifted off the ground and soared out into space. Numerous small specks were detached from the third ship. They were obviously trying to get as far and as fast as possible away from the slowly sinking ship.

The plan had worked. The Springers had failed to find the bomb!

At the moment of the landing a sharp jolt made the ground vibrate. The bomb of the HORL was detonated.

Nobody doubted that the explosion of the bomb would leave anything but molecular and atomic particles of the proud Springer ship. The fuse had been set to react with the artificial elements which were continuously produced by the fusion reactors of the ship.

Tiff held his breath for a second when he felt the ground shaking. Nobody noticed it – except possibly Pucky. But Pucky said nothing and Tiff was grateful.

Tiff felt no different than a man watching an aeroplane crash with a load of atom bombs on board. He would do the natural thing of holding his breath, waiting for the bombs to explode at the moment of impact, although knowing the bombs could not possibly explode no matter how severe the shock they suffered, since the fuse of an atom bomb is a much more complicated mechanism.

Tiff was in the same situation. He was well aware that the other Arkon bombs could not be made to go off by exploding one of them close by. The firing mechanism was more intricate than that to allow such a disaster. All that could happen was that the other bombs would be blown to bits without releasing their energy.

Nevertheless Tiff had been afraid that a quirk could somehow cause the detonation of the HORL'S whole load of bombs. This would have meant the end of Snowman. But no such thing had happened.

They put the two girls aboard the auxiliary ships as well as the untiring stalwart Aubrey. The robot had reported that nothing particular had happened in the meantime.

The girls were very curious but Pucky pressed on, demanding that his crew leave the danger zone as quickly as possible. He arranged a meeting place 1800 miles to the south with Tiff and Eberhardt piloting the two crafts. The ships took off at once.

Pucky jumped as soon as he lost sight of them and arrived at the meeting place at the same instant. He made good use of the time. Perry Rhodan was waiting for information from him.

'Pucky is calling you, sir!' John Marshall announced.

'Let's hear what he has to say!' Rhodan replied eagerly.

Marshall seemed to listen inwardly. Two minutes later he lifted his head and said: 'Pucky and the cadets were in danger of being blasted to death with the planet. They've weathered the situation by taking appropriate measures. An enemy ship has been destroyed in the process. Pucky has attempted to keep the number of victims low by issuing a warning in time.'

'Good for him!' Rhodan broke in. 'Go on!'

'In the course of the operations Pucky has been able to ascertain valuable information from the commander of the largest Springer ship.

'First: All hostile action taken against Terra stemmed from one single ship, the ORLA, which captured Tifflor and the K-9. Only during the final days, when it looked as if the captain of the ORLA was no longer in control of the situation, were other warships summoned.

'Secondly: The captain of the ORLA has assigned special robots as his agents on Terra . . .'

Marshall paused for a moment.

'That's why our telepaths were unable to detect any of the enemy agents,' Rhodan murmured.

Marshall continued: 'The robots resemble humans and can only be distinguished by their small fusion motors . . .'

'Excellent!' Rhodan interrupted again.

'Furthermore, the Springers do not yet know exactly how to judge the Earth and its civilization. The information they've received from the robot agents and the experience they've made with our ships in space don't seem to jibe . . .'

'No wonder!' Rhodan laughed.

'Thus they're inclined towards the opinion that Terra should first be studied closer. If it turns out that the planet is underdeveloped the Springers intend to establish a trading base there. If mankind on Earth, however, has reached a level comparable with the Springers, we're to be punished for violating the monopoly of the Springers by carrying on interstellar trade.'

Rhodan was still smiling. 'We'll make it rough on them!' he chuckled. Then he passed on his own instructions to Pucky:

'The *Stardust* is going to leave the Beta–Albireo sector in a few hours. *Terra* and the *Solar System* will remain here. It's necessary to equip the *Stardust* with new armaments which will enable us to withstand the onslaught of the hostile armada in this sector without other help.

'The *Stardust* will be gone a maximum of four weeks. *Terra* and the *Solar System* have orders to keep the enemy in the Beta–Albireo sector at bay, inflict losses on him and support our team on Snowman by all means at our disposal. There'll be at least one telepath on board the two ships at all times.

'Pucky and the cadets are instructed to continue their task on Snowman, to collect further information and to keep out of the clutches of the Springers.'

After Rhodan had finished his message Marshall transmitted it word for word.

The patrol crafts arrived a few minutes later. They touched down near the mouse-beaver. Aubrey was the first to climb out. Then came the girls and the cadets were last.

Tiff was eager to check the thermometer. 'Only

minus 112° F,' he murmured in surprise. 'It's really much warmer here.'

'We're fairly close to the equator,' Pucky explained.

Pucky had waited in a sort of valley. It was an almost circular basin of over 300 feet diameter completely surrounded by gentle white hills with peaks rising between 150 and 300 feet above the level of the valley.

The place could not have been selected better if Pucky had explored Snowman before. On the northern slope of one of the hills to the south gaped a hole bigger than a man. Pucky had already investigated it and found a tunnel leading from there deep into the hill.

'It's a natural for a hide-out,' Pucky pointed out. 'Of course we'll have to camouflage the entrance so it can't be seen so easily. But first we'll have to enlarge it enough to hold the two patrol ships. After that I believe the Springers will have a hard time catching up with us.'

They went to work at once. Tiff flew back once more to the cave Aubrey had dug out of the rock to pick up those of Pucky's supplies they had been able to salvage on their hasty flight from the shelter.

Tiff meanwhile had already determined that the most vital equipment had been hauled out, as for instance the parts of a miniature power station which was adequate for providing the comfort of light and heat in their new abode. They had saved weapons and foodstuff as well as an efficient hypercom transceiver with the necessary components for condensed transmissions, frequency integration and similar secret devices for clandestine operations in a hostile country.

When Tiff returned Aubrey had already widened the tunnel sufficiently to let the auxiliary ships be moved inside. A hundred feet from the outside and covered by a dense hill they ran little risk of being detected.

Farther inside, approximately below the peak of the hill, they built their own quarters. The power station was quickly installed. Ice covered the surface of Snowman to a depth of at least 60 feet but here they were below that depth and the walls turned to rock. With the heat ray of his thermobeamer Aubrey smoothed the glittering cold rockwalls and in a remarkably short time created five chambers in a row.

Only after the job was finished did Pucky finally settle down and acquaint the cadets and the girls with the instructions from Rhodan.

Hifield frowned as he listened to the news. He appeared on the verge of making one of his famous nasty remarks. Observing the telltale signs, Tiff forestalled him by saying, 'We'll be comfortable here for four weeks.'

Pucky agreed and Hifield stared at the floor.

'There's something else I have to tell you,' Pucky said, and his tone was so peculiar that it immediately aroused everyone's interest. 'For some time now I've been receiving by telepathy the strangest emanations. As if there is somebody in the vicinity who is unconscious or in a state of hibernation. I'd like to know who it is. If the Springers will keep off our tails long enough' – and with the mouse-beaver it was more than a figure of speech – 'we can try to get to the bottom of this curious phenomenon.'

The Springers kept peace temporarily. Not a single enemy ship neared the hideout. Whether this was because Etztak had halted his pursuit or they were simply unable to track them down, no one could say, but the upshot was that they were left alone and this was of paramount importance.

Pucky applied himself with great diligence to the search for the somnolent impulses. However, the source could not be determined because the emanations were so diffuse, coming from varying directions and in fluctuating intensities. Mystery of mysteries! What might happen when the sleeper woke . . . or the sleepers waked?

Hifield, in the meantime, reverted to his old obnoxious behaviour pattern. To his previous inane rivalries he now added jealously. Because Mildred was showing her preference for Tiff, Hifield was so miffed that he failed to observe that Felicita Kergonen somehow was attracted to *him*.

Hifield taunted Tiff and Tiff teased him in return but Hifield never caught on till Klaus Eberhardt told him one day, 'If I were as dumb as you I'd lock myself up for two days without opening my silly trap once!'

Pucky watched the antics and quarrels of the cadets with a brain born for amusement. He was glad these hotblooded young Terrestrials had a period of rest and peace so that they could engage in more human problems.

An end was bound to come soon enough when idle play would turn once again to imminent peril.

The day – or night – when Etztak would strike his next blow.

When the Springer enemy would spring again!

THE FOREVER WAR

Joe Haldeman

Winner of the 1976 Nebula and Hugo Awards.

Earth has been fighting for its life against an alien civilization which simply will not negotiate.

The elite of Earth's young people are trained to fight a war fought at speeds approaching that of light. Relativity comes into play. A group of young people will leave the Earth aged 27 and return *two of their years later* to find that the Earth and war have moved on by fifty, a hundred, maybe several hundred years.

Making brilliant use of this paradox and the well nigh impossible logistics of fighting such a war, Joe Haldeman has given us the most impressive SF novel of the past ten years – an instant classic.

THE MOTE IN GOD'S EYE

Larry Niven and Jerry Pournelle

An alien space ship, using some motive power unknown to man comes sailing, into the outer reaches of the solar system.

The team sent to intercept it accidentally destroy it, but its course has been recorded accurately enough to extrapolate its point of origin.

A team of scientists, escorted by the most powerful battleship in Earth's space fleet is sent to contact this newly discovered civilization. What they find is at once the most exciting and tragic destiny ever to be suffered by sentient beings.

'The best novel about human beings making first contact with intelligent but utterly nonhuman aliens I have ever seen, and possibly the finest science fiction novel I have ever read.'
– Robert A. Heinlein.

'A spellbinder, a swashbuckler . . . and best of all a brilliant new approach to that fascinating problem – first contact with aliens.'
– Frank Herbert.

J BARNICOAT
CASH SALES DEPT.,
P.O. BOX 11
FALMOUTH
CORNWALL TR10 9EN

Please send me the following titles

Quantity	SBN	Title	Amount
______			______
______			______
______			______
______			______
______			______
			______
		TOTAL	======

Please enclose a cheque or postal order made out to FUTURA PUBLICATIONS LIMITED for the amount due, including 10p per book to allow for postage and packing. Orders will take about three weeks to reach you and we cannot accept responsibility for orders containing cash.

PLEASE PRINT CLEARLY

NAME ....

ADDRESS ....

....